NORFOLK

Noleen Jordan

ISBN: 9781511633499
ISBN: 1511633492
Library of Congress Control Number: 2015908468
CreateSpace Independent Publishing Platform
North Charleston, South Carolina

Also by this author:

Shwedagon

Life has taught me to have a Plan B,
Friends encourage me to see what I can see,
Family inspire me to be the best that I can be,
But you, my love, just allow me to be me.

To see a detailed map of Norfolk Island and other visitor information, please visit this website:

http://www.norfolkisland.com.au/

CONTENTS

1

KINGSTON

"**W**oody? Have you seen these waves?" Megan Woodward called to her husband.

"Yes, love, they're bloody enormous! I haven't seen waves that high at Slaughter Bay for a decade. Must be the cyclone over New Caledonia pushing south—it'll leave a high-pressure system in the area for a day or so," Woody replied.

Alex Woodward, known as Woody to his mates, was a native of Norfolk Island. He ran a small farm perched on the hillside above Queen Elizabeth Lookout. The farm overlooked the horseshoe shape of the popular beach at Emily Bay. His view was unimpeded across the old penal settlement of Kingston, to Slaughter Bay and Flagstaff in the distance. A single, perfectly formed

Norfolk pine was centre of frame in the outlook to the east of the farm. The golf course sat beneath Woody's property, adjacent to the renovated heritage cottages, just a short drive back from the cemetery.

"There's a whole crowd of locals down at the pier watching the waves. A bit of excitement for the week," laughed Megan. "Should be some good photos, but it wrecks the weekend's fishing plans."

"Yeah, I know. It sucks, but what do you do?" Woody groaned.

Woody and Megan had bought the old farm when they married thirty-five years ago. Their little cottage had one of the best outlooks on the island. Their front windows looked across neighbouring Nepean Island to Philip Island in the distance. South across the Pacific Ocean beyond the horizon, their nearest neighbours were in New Zealand, some eleven hundred kilometres away.

World-famous Norfolk pine trees lined the fore-shore of Emily Bay, stretching across toward Slaughter Bay and encircling the green fields known as the Common.

The usually calm waters of Emily Bay were be-ing whipped into a liquid fury. Tumultuous waves hammered the rock shelf that formed a barrier to the open sea. Around from the point where Lone Pine guarded the beachfront, waves in excess of ten metres crashed incessantly onto the rocks across the shoreline along Slaughter Bay. At the western end of Kingston, the sea churned grinding waves up over the concrete pier, covering the top of the crane with each successive surge.

While the seas were rough, the weather was surprisingly calm. The day was warm, and the water was a pleasant twenty-four degrees Celsius. Families paddled in the shallow water along the long sandy beach that edged Emily Bay. A boy chased a dog chasing a Frisbee along the sand. A tour bus disgorged passengers along the headland near Lone Pine.

Picnickers enjoyed the shaded grass area along the beachfront at the ruins of the old Salt House. Swimmers ventured out to the wooden pontoon anchored in the middle of the bay. It was a welcome spot to sunbake, and teenagers dived into the clear water around it. Snorkelers chased tropical parrot fish through the seaweed nearby. Trumpet fish explored the toes of the snorkelers, often nipping them in the process.

Life made its normal daily transition in this piece of paradise in the middle of the Pacific Ocean.

Waves in Emily Bay were uncommon. Usually the rock shelf that kept sharks out also kept the sea from rippling the waters in the bay. Today, the water in the bay was rough. The waves that were crashing over the rock shelf had stirred up debris and tossed chunks of dead coral across the sandy floor of the bay.

Crews in outrigger canoes finished their training session, ready for the annual Ocean Racing Classic around the island. Other canoes and kayaks were hidden among the trees just behind the beachfront, ready for their next outing.

There would be no glass-bottom boat tour today. They needed calm water for that.

Norfolk Island had no natural harbour, no port for cruise ships, no dock for merchant ships or tenders, no moorings for yachts, no anchorage at all. Boats had to be lifted into the water and then lifted out again after use. Vessels were carried away and stored until needed again. The last quote to build a harbour had come in at $62 million—an impossible amount for the locals to amass with so few residents to pay for it.

Instead, the locals made do with two concrete piers on either side of the island. Each pier was fitted with a crane that was manually operated. The coupling hook on the crane was used to lift each vessel into the water by way of a reciprocal lifting hook fitted to the boat. It was quite a sight for anyone who had not witnessed it before. It was like stepping back in time to another era. Life was simple.

Once a month, a cargo ship called in to the island to replenish any supplies ordered from the mainland. When the ship was due, a decision had to be made. Which pier would offer the calmest water on the day of unloading? There were only two piers, so the choice was limited. Cascade Bay on the north shore was the usual winner.

Generally, though, the waters around Norfolk were calm. In one or two places, the sea current pushed roughly against the rugged cliffs along the coast. These areas made good scuba diving spots but were not recommended swimming areas.

On cargo day, the ship anchored about a kilometre off the coast. The whaleboats would be launched by crane. Then they would be tied together, and long wooden logs would be lashed across the pair of boats to support the pallets of stock being collected. The twin vessels would then motor out to the ship as one. Palletised cargo would be craned from the ship onto these old whaleboats. When they returned to the pier, the pallets were craned up and loaded onto the waiting utes and flat-top trucks. The process was repeated until the cargo ship was empty. This could take all day, depending on the sea conditions.

When new cars had been ordered, they too came ashore on these whaleboats. It was quite a sight to see a car balanced atop them. Even more impressive was seeing two whaleboats tethered together with a minibus balanced across the width of them. They didn't often lose a vehicle overboard!

The cargo ship *Enid* had left Norfolk a week ago, so no other vessel was due for another three weeks.

The fishing vessels were usually launched from the northern pier early in the morning. On their return to the pier, the fish were cleaned and the burley tossed overboard to the sharks that followed them in to the pier. If you were on the pier when the trawlers returned, you could photograph the sharks through clear water that was three metres deep.

Today there would be no fishing trips, due to the sea conditions. Tourists were being asked to rebook their deep-sea fishing adventures for another day. The famous fish fry had been postponed tonight. You cannot cook what you have not caught!

In the major downtown area of Norfolk Island was the shopping village known as Burnt Pine Township. The small number of shops that stretched along either side of these two blocks had to service the entire population.

Archie entered the Tour Office through the back door. "Olive, I'll just leave the paperwork on your desk." He called to the woman at the front counter. "That's the last tour group for the day so I'm taking the minibus home with me. I'll top it up with petrol on the way back tomorrow."

"Yeah, sure Archie." Olive replied, turning to look at him. "You OK? You seem a bit agitated."

"Oh, I still get cranky with some of the bloody stupid questions these tourists ask. It's the same thing every bloody tour." Archie complained. "Most people are really nice, but I swear, there's one in every crowd that just drives me bloody nuts!"

"What have they done this time Archie?" Olive treated his comment with amusement. She was smirking, knowing she had heard this complaint from the old man a thousand times.

"So today, I'm out at St Barnabas Church, explaining how the chapel design was based on the up-turned hull of a boat, right? When this stupid woman asks me - *which boat*!" Archie was building up steam as he began to vent his displeasure on poor little Olive. "They just don't get it, do they? It's any bloody boat – that's why they call it architect designed. It wasn't built from a bloody shipwreck – seriously!"

Archie growled. "This morning some kid asked me - *what colour is a grey gum?*" Archie was furling his brow in despair.

Olive was happy to stir Archie up. "My favourite is when they ask you when the first Norfolk pine tree was planted!"

"Yeah, they think I'm bloody Methuselah. As if anybody was here - it was an uninhabited island when the British arrived two hundred years ago and the trees were already here. Honestly!" Archie started shaking his head in a show of frustration.

Olive thought better of letting him brood on the subject so she made an excuse to use the phone, leaving Archie to wave goodbye and head home. Olive knew better than letting him start another conversation. He was known as Have-a-Chat for a reason.

While Archie paid no income tax to the Australian government, he also got no pension from them. This was the norm on Norfolk. You had to provide for your own retirement. There was no Social Security here, no dole, no pension when you retired.

Archie spent a few hours a week driving tourist minibuses for the local tour operator. That supplemented his small income from his life savings. It also gave him a chance to talk to some new faces each week. Have-a-Chat loved sharing his knowledge of Norfolk with the tourists.

Some nights he also got involved with the local fish fry the islanders put on for the tourists. It was a good night. They would set up a barbecue out at Puppy's Point just above Flat Rock. Then they would cook, and the tourists would eat for hours on end.

They only stopped cooking when the tourists complained of full bellies. The fresh seafood was always special on Norfolk.

As night fell, the only light source in the downtown area was the occasional restaurant and shop front. Apart from a handful of streetlights at the only round-about in town, there was no other public lighting.

The population of Norfolk was typically around fifteen hundred permanent local residents. This number had reduced in recent years. The woes of the global financial crisis had stretched to some of the businesses on the island. Owners had sold where they could and moved back to the mainland. Other shop fronts now sat empty; no new tenants could be found. The current population was down to just over a thousand permanent residents.

This number was boosted by the weekly influx of tourists from Australia and New Zealand. Half the islanders were involved in the tourist industry in some way. They rented out tourist accommodations, drove tour buses, organised day tours and fishing trips. If that was not enough, they performed at the nighttime entertainment and local shows.

The island could accommodate up to five hundred tourists a week. After that, the island's resources were stretched. Tourist numbers were also down this week due to the cyclone that had brought summer to a close.

Norfolk was essentially self-sufficient. Rich volcanic soil had allowed the islanders to grow their own fruit and vegetables. Farms raised animals—sheep, pigs, cattle, and chickens—that provided flavoursome meats. Fruits and veggies ripened naturally, so they were full of nutrients and flavour. Food was organic and healthy, but seasonal. Lettuce; sweet, juicy tomatoes; and potatoes were available year round—otherwise, the seasons dictated what was served on plates in homes and diners. Roadside stalls offered fresh produce and homegrown honey at the farm gate. Honesty boxes were the only method of payment.

Supermarkets would not carry apples from Tasmania, or mangoes from Queensland, or any fresh produce from overseas. Import of fruit and vegetables was strictly forbidden. Islanders could not risk the introduction of foreign pests that had the potential to wipe out local crops. Sniffer dogs met you at the airport to make sure you were not carrying fruit, vegetables, or plant matter from foreign countries.

Out near the Hundred Acre Woods, the home of the cattle known as Norfolk Blue, the restaurant served some of the best steaks around. In town, there were some other really great places to dine.

Locals supplied their own water through underground tanks at each property. Electricity was expensive if bought from the town grid, so most homes had solar power. As a result, they paid no council rates, no land taxes, and no water rates.

There was no postal service—you collected your own mail when you went to town. There was no rubbish collection service—you took your own rubbish to the town collection site. Here, the rubbish was sorted into recyclables to be shipped back to the Australian mainland, or rubbish that could be incinerated at the waste site, Headstone Tip. Anything else became compost or fish food.

This was a small village community that took care of itself. In return for this, the residents paid no income tax. There was, however, a local consumption tax of 12 percent to cover administration costs on the island. This also funded the supply of general services necessary to daily life—roads, hospitals, and a community hall, to name a few.

Islanders had to support themselves, as there were no social security payments given out by the Australian government to Norfolk Islanders. Residents had to plan for their retirement—superannuation was nonexistent unless you had your own savings plan for old age.

The Heritage area of Kingston was supported by a strong network of local museums and other tourist experiences that raised vital funds. National Parks got financial assistance from the New South Wales National Parks and Wildlife Service back on the mainland. There was very little financial support from the Australian government.

As a result, the roads were becoming pockmarked—there were no funds to continually repair them. Only the roads in Burnt Pine Township were maintained.

The small hospital tended to the medical needs of the community. This extended to dental care as well. There was no government-funded Medicare available here, so residents paid for their own health insurance costs. For any major surgical needs, patients had to travel to the mainland. Emergency air evacuation could cost $25,000, so it was best avoided. Tourists were advised to get travel insurance before they arrived on Norfolk.

Local services offered a good array of shopping for tourists and locals alike. While the majority of goods were imported, there was no import duty added to the landed cost. The island had become something of a shopper's paradise, with prices very competitive to those on the mainland.

Tourists found it hard to get used to the village lifestyle, with shops closing at lunchtime Saturday and staying closed all day Sunday. Some shops even closed Wednesday afternoon as well.

A local radio station kept residents up to date with regional news and snippets from the mainland. The weekly newspaper was referred to as 'two minutes of silence' because that was how long it took to read it.

There was a commercial airport that accepted flights five days a week. Air New Zealand offered one flight each way to Sydney on Friday and Monday—the flight from Brisbane arrived each Tuesday and Saturday. The only direct flight to Auckland left each Sunday. Apart from that, the only traffic at the airport was some small planes that used Norfolk as a refuelling stop when crossing the Pacific. Otherwise, the airport sat idle.

Built by the Australian government during World War II as a strategic refuelling base in the South Pacific, the airport was the second lifeline of the island. Online shopping and emergency supplies arrived on planes from Australia and New Zealand, along with tourists and returning residents.

Fresh milk had to be flown in, as there was no pasteurisation plant on Norfolk and unpasteurised milk could not legally be sold to the public. At $8.37 a litre, fresh milk was a luxury that most could not afford. Locals had learnt to drink their tea black unless they had their own cow, otherwise they bought the cheaper long-life milk at $2.36 a litre. Other imported foods were equally expensive. It was not uncommon for residents returning from holidays on the mainland to bring back suitcases full of tinned and packet groceries—even toilet paper. Grocery prices on Norfolk proved to be frightening for tourists. Locals saw it as the price you paid to live in paradise. They avoided the cost of purchased goods by growing their own where possible.

Petrol was shipped in and currently sold for $2.65 a litre, which was more than double the price charged in Sydney. While the island was small, even the tiniest car could chew through fifty dollars' worth of petrol a week at those prices.

Today's flight from Sydney returned 62 locals and brought only a 129 tourists. The departing cyclone had reduced tourist numbers this week. The flight back to Sydney took 19 locals for specialist medical treatments. There were another 189 tourists going home to Sydney and beyond.

The rest of the plane was filled with 87 locals who had flown out for their annual holiday in the big smoke. Locals cherished island life, but at least once a year, they felt the need to escape for a while. It wasn't long before they craved island life again, usually within a week of arriving in the big smoke. They were all thankful to be able to return to the peaceful existence they enjoyed on this subtropical island.

Norfolk was a relatively small speck in the middle of the Pacific. It measured only eight kilometres by five and sat fourteen hundred kilometres east of the Australian coast. Its closest neighbour was seven hundred kilometres away in New Caledonia to the north.

While Norfolk Island was an external territory that belonged to Australia, even Australians needed passports to land there. Australians were often surprised to discover they needed passports inside their own country—it was weird.

The Australian colonists had twice tried to establish a penal colony on Norfolk. They had not been able to preserve an ongoing community.

The original residents of Norfolk were from Pitcairn Island, far away to the east near the coast of South America. Survivors of the mutiny on the *Bounty* hid on Pitcairn Island for many years, until discovered by American sailors. By that time, they had multiplied and their population had outgrown Pitcairn. They were offered Norfolk Island as a way of populating this twice-deserted penal colony.

There were many descendants of the original Pitcairn Islanders living on Norfolk. Pitcairn natives had produced a new generation when they procreated with mutineers from the *Bounty*. It was common for them to adopt one of the names of the mutiny's leader in the process. So, one Fletcher Christian had shared his name among the Pitcairn natives long before they moved to Norfolk. As a result, the Norfolk phone book was full of Fletchers and Christians. Sheer numbers of families sharing the same two surnames had the potential to cause mass confusion when referring to the local phone book, so nicknames were printed in the book instead. In fact, the book was ruled by nicknames—Dingo, Digger, Baz, Meggsie. Rarely was there an actual legally recognised name in the phone book.

Administration of the island was shared between the government-appointed chief minister and the Council of Nine, the locally elected legislative assembly. It consisted of nine elected descendants of the Pitcairners, and they were responsible for making decisions on spending and local political issues.

Recent changes of legislation meant natives of Australia and New Zealand were now allowed to buy property on Norfolk and potentially apply for residency.

Anyone else could stay for a maximum of 120 days only.

As the night sky darkened, the stars began to emerge. The twinkling constellations above Emily Bay were all the more noticeable because of the lack of electric streetlights across Norfolk Island. Thousands upon thousands of stars were visible in the night sky—too many to count. It was a stunningly impressive sight if you were reclined on the grass at the golf course looking skyward. There were more stars than one had ever imagined possible.

The administrative offices in the historic area of Kingston were partially lit at night but deserted. Farther along the road, the heritage cottages occupied by the chief minister and the chief doctor fell silent. Occupants retired for the evening; lights were turned out; there was no traffic in the area at night. The golf course was deserted at this hour.

Townships typically cause reduced visibility of the night sky above them. At Kingston, the only lights were from the few houses on the hillside overlooking the heritage site. On the road past the cemetery, there was little beyond Bloody Bridge to interfere with viewing the night sky.

Near the Kingston pier, the museum buildings and ranger's cottage sat silent for the night ahead.

The restaurant, perched on the hill that overlooked Kingston, had finally packed up for the night; its lights were now extinguished.

The cattle that grazed freely on the Common were the only things that moved in the area. Any local could own cattle and get permission for them to roam freely around the island. The cattle were branded with the owner's mark to make identification easy when it came time for slaughtering these beasts.

The animals were kept out of town and out of gardens by a series of cattle grids around the island. Cattle could graze freely down on the Common. They would not wander far because the cattle grids isolated them to designated areas. The poddy calves had taken their last milk for the day. Cattle and their calves started to settle in for the night.

It would be hours before the roosters began crowing, but when they started, they would cock-a-doodle over several hours. Tourists often wanted to hunt them down and destroy them—they were unused to the real sounds of a rural lifestyle and resented being woken at 4.00 a.m.

The fowl joined the ducks as they retreated to the old windmill area around the dam at the bottom of Taylors Road.

Slaughter Bay fell silent, and the waves started to quieten after a vicious afternoon.

There was no street lighting along the beachfront, nor any along the pier. The few cars that had lingered to watch the rollicking waves had long since gone home. Waves had started to subside, and the area was once again returned to its calm self. The beachfront lovers' lane was now deserted.

There was no one to witness the wooden boat that limped unexpectedly around Point Hunter. It snuck past the entrance to Emily Bay and into the waters of Sydney Bay just beyond the rock shelf.

There was no one to count the 146 souls onboard.

2

ARRIVALS

The *Dragoon* was a traditional Indonesian schooner. It was a typical two-masted boat built from ironwood with decks of teak. These were the favoured fishing vessels of the Indonesian fleet.

When they had first seen the *Dragoon*, it was only partially built. Designed more like a ketch than a dhow, these sturdy vessels were often seen on the ocean. Usually their fishing nets were extended, waiting for a major catch.

The shipyard in South Sulawesi in Indonesia wanted to continue to fit it out with an interior suited to housing a crew of eight, with the usual space set aside for the catch, nets, galley, and supplies.

These people had other ideas.

By eliminating most of the interior fit out, as well as the masts, they could accommodate more than a hundred people for the seven-thousand-kilometre journey. The schooner would motor from Indonesia to Norfolk around the top of Papua New Guinea to avoid detection from the Australian border protection agencies. This course ensured they would not be spotted by Australian aerial patrols.

They had been told to land on Australian soil to claim asylum.

Refugees were required to pay $3,000 per person for their share of the finished vessel—every man, woman, and child who wanted passage paid the same price. This was a massive windfall for the boat builder, who would normally have sold the completed vessel for US$100,000. Instead, he would reap nearly $450,000. That made it worth his while to stall the original purchaser and sell to these people instead.

All he had to do was supply the Mitsubishi six-cylinder D-14 190-horsepower engine; a Dompeng 120-horsepower 7.5-kilovolt generator; a GPS; a compass; a 3.5-metre rubber dinghy that seated six; a 15-horsepower Yamaha motor; just fifteen lifejackets; and enough fuel to cover the distance. He would supply no spare fuel for contingencies.

The only other tool the refugees had requested was a map of Norfolk Island. Google provided one in just a couple of clicks. The boat builder had downloaded it from the Internet.

The schooner was twenty-four meters long with a keel length of eleven and a half metres. The beam was four and a quarter metres, and the boat pulled a draft of one and three-quarter metres. The deck length of nearly twenty metres allowed rotation of passengers above and below deck on a roster system. It had also given them space to bring their few worldly possessions along with them.

All the risk remained with the refugees.

The boat builder would teach them to operate and repair the motor, the generator, and the GPS.

There was barely one square metre per person. Ablutions were performed over the side, no exceptions.

It was a long journey and far from easy, but considering the life they were escaping, anything else was worth the effort.

They fished from the deck to feed the passengers and managed to collect enough rainwater to supplement the supplies brought onboard. They snuck into a cove on the northern side of Papua New Guinea to top up their dwindling supplies and gathered tropical fruit growing wild in the rainforest. A freshwater crocodile made a welcome meal for the refugees, though for a while, it was almost the other way around!

Hopes were kept high as they counted out the days, living in squalid conditions on the *Dragoon*. They were used to hardship; their own homelands had been destroyed by wars, politics, and religion. This, at least, was a means to an end. There was the hope of a new life on the horizon.

They had been at sea for seventy-one days when the winds from Cyclone Zena pushed them off course. It proved to be a blessing really, because they missed the worst of the storm, which had decimated Noumea in New Caledonia just five days ago.

The downside for the refugees was the time it took to get back on course. The sea conditions, the wind, and the rain had been atrocious for weeks as a result of the cyclone season. They had been totally unprepared. None of them had come from countries where the wet season was a consideration.

Inexperience showed, but they survived in spite of their lack of local knowledge.

They were all safe, though they were in need of a good bath and fresh food and clothes. The luxury of a real bed would have been a welcome treat.

The crew missed sighting the pier at Cascade Bay to the north of the island. The pier sat in a tiny, unlit cove that was less than fifty metres long. They sailed farther south around the eastern side of the island but found nowhere else to attempt a landing. All they saw were sheer cliffs.

No one onboard thought about the lack of lighting on Norfolk. They almost sailed past the island in the night. There were no lighthouses to mark the edge of the cliffs. Most of the farmhouses were inland, away from the coast, unseen across rolling hills and valleys.

Those homes that were close to the sea were unlit by the time the schooner came alongside the island's eastern seaboard at 3.25 a.m.

Another half hour passed while they sailed down the east coast in the moonlight, and then they turned the vessel westward around Point Hunter, near Nepean Island.

GPS was great, but you still needed to see the land to find somewhere to go ashore. It was only the lighting around the grounds of the historic settlement of

Kingston that confirmed the location of the island's main beach. Someone glimpsed it as the schooner came alongside Nepean Island to the south of Norfolk. The boat was now running on fumes.

As the *Dragoon* neared the headland, the rock shelf came into sight of those standing on the deck. The cove known as Emily Bay was hidden from view. Waves crashed over the rock ledge, which led them to believe this was the edge of the island. The moonlight showed land abutting the rock shelf.

In the excitement of reaching their destination, a handful of passengers decided to jump from the ship, expecting to land in shallow water on the rock ledge. Instead they were thrown into the ocean as the rough seas bounced the vessel over the next wave. They panicked, not knowing how to swim. . Their arms were bleeding from being scraped on the rocks while trying to get a foothold. Two men clutching small children found their footing and scrambled onto the rocks, cutting their bare feet on the dead coral embedded in the rock ledge.

A woman jumped overboard behind them, mimicking their movements in an attempt to get to land. As she did so, the child she was cradling slipped from her arms into the water. Her screams pierced the air but could not be heard above the crashing waves. The child was lost to the sea in the darkness of the night. His body was dragged under the boat and out of sight of his sobbing, panicked mother. The men grabbed the woman's arms and dragged her onto the rock shelf. They pulled her up alongside them onto the rocks of the headland near Lone Pine.

Then they dragged her up onto the flat area above the rock shelf, where she collapsed, exhausted, onto the grass. Her husband wrapped his arms around her to stop her from throwing herself back into the sea to join her dead child. They shivered in the light rain left behind from the storm front.

The little group watched as the *Dragoon* sailed on to the middle of the bay in front of them.

When the captain could make out the location of the pier at Kingston, he ordered the anchors dropped. There were lights around a cluster of buildings not far from the beachfront, so that held some promise.

The crew of *Dragoon* threw its anchor into the waters of Sydney Bay, just over a kilometre off Slaughter Bay.

Named after the Old English habit of running words together, the description for "slow water" had become Slaughter Bay. It could be as treacherous as the name implied, irrespective of its literal translation.

Their only dinghy was launched, and the landing party set off to find a safe place to bring the others ashore.

For the first time in weeks, they were off the *Dragoon* and breathing the islands fresh air.

They had arrived.

At the Flagstaff end of Slaughter Bay, the Kingston pier jutted into the ocean over the rock shelf. It could be tricky to manoeuvre vessels around the rocks. Locals were wary of using rubber dinghies lest they snag on the coral outcrops that were embedded in the rock shelf.

The small group of refugees steered the dinghy toward the outline of the crane simply out of curiosity. The map showed a landing jetty of some sort, but they had no idea of the condition they would find it in.

Searching for beach access proved impossible. The rock shelf prevented them coming closer to the shore.

It was high tide, so they had the best chance of negotiating the sharp rocks beneath them.

As they approached the pier, they realised it was a concrete structure. They had hoped to find a floating pontoon that would rise and fall with the tide to match the level of the water.

"This is not going to be easy to land." Fadi said with concern. "The deck is a metre above the level of the water."

"Fadi, I will give you a lift onto the platform," called Abbud, captain of the *Dragoon*. "And then you can see if you can find some steps somewhere, or even a way across to the beach."

Abbud hoisted Fadi up onto his bent knee, then put his hands beneath Fadi's bum and thrust him skyward. Fadi landed with little aplomb onto the hard concrete deck.

The crane loomed overhead.

They wondered at the hook mechanism that now dangled above them. They could not have known that it was useless to them without a reciprocal hook on their dinghy.

Fadi walked the length of the pier in the moonlight; dawn was still an hour away.

He could see no break in the rock shelf that would allow them to land passengers directly onto the beach. It would be slow going bringing everyone from the vessel onto the pier using the little dinghy.

At the end of the pier, Fadi found the road that led around the buildings near the jetty. There was a relic of a whaleboat farther along the road past the museum, but he could not find anyone to help them. The place was deserted.

In the distance, Fadi heard a cow mooing and stopped to check the distance between him and the animal. He could see the buildings along the foreshore more clearly now. According to their map, the ruins of the jail were not far away. Other buildings rose out of the darkness on the other side of the huge paddock. There was little light to show him what was beyond that.

He could see a large building with some floodlights about four hundred metres away across the field where the cows sat.

He relayed this information to Abbud. "Shall I go there?"

"Not yet; I want everyone ashore first." Abbud had brought them there safely, so he wanted them on terra firma before the locals knew they had arrived.

Fadi helped unload the dinghy of its human cargo. These were the first refugees to step ashore on Norfolk.

Abbud turned the dinghy around and returned for the many passengers to be taken off the *Dragoon*. They would set up a shuttle to go back and forth until everyone was off the schooner.

Low tide was imminent. This made it harder to lift passengers from the dinghy up onto the concrete pier. The water level had dropped another forty-five centimetres in the last hour.

Abbud turned the dinghy around for another run out to the *Dragoon*. There was a sudden catch underneath the little rubber boat as it snagged on the coral protruding from the rock shelf. The thick rubber was sliced along the underside at a length of about eight centimetres. There was a noticeable hiss, accompanied by a rapid rise of bubbles along the side. *Damn!*

He could not risk another load of passengers lest the little vessel deflated rapidly. He had no choice but to turn the dinghy back to the pier.

Fadi caught the tethering rope and pulled the dinghy in close to the pier. He tied it off to secure it.

Abbud's frame felt like a dead weight in the dinghy as Fadi hauled him up onto the pier.

The two men discussed their immediate problem as they walked the length of the pier to join those already ashore.

"What do you want us to do now?" Fadi asked.

"We have no choice; we have to ask for help." Abbud was resigned to it.

They would need to get assistance now to land the last of their number. They had been running the dinghy out and back for nearly two hours, the sound of the motor muffled by the crashing waves. It was slow going when you could only bring back five at a time.

There were over a hundred who had come ashore already. The newcomers had wandered across to the paddock to stretch their legs and admire the cows and chickens on the Common. Newcomers discussed slaughtering their first fresh meat in months. They were waiting for Abbud or Fadi to tell them what to do next.

The headlights coming down the hill were an early surprise. Dawn had not yet cracked the horizon. They had thought they had more time on their side. Now they would have to face the authorities.

At 5.45 a.m., Reilly Reid pulled his Toyota four-wheel drive out of his garage and headed down Taylors Road toward Emily Bay. He liked to get his daily run over and done with before the day started. As head park ranger, he had lots to occupy his time each day. He was responsible for more park rangers than there were police on the island.

By parking on Quality Row, he had worked out an easy five-kilometre jog that would bring him back to his vehicle in less than thirty minutes. The route would take him past the administrator's cottage, down around the golf course, and then returning across the back of Emily Bay. He would then swing past Slaughter Bay and back up to the Common. It was a great way to start the day, and he would be home in time for breakfast with his wife at 6.30 a.m.

Nothing could have prepared him for the crowd loitering on the Common in front of the Barracks.

"What the f…?" he cussed to himself as he slammed his foot onto the brake.

Rubbing his eyes, he confirmed he was not hallucinating. There were dozens of people staring back at him through his car headlights.

"Jesus. Where did they come from?" He hit the anchors hard, and the car screeched to a halt sending gravel and dust skyward.

He grabbed his mobile phone off the seat next to him and called the police station.

"Sergeant Parish" was the sleepy response when the phone was finally answered. It had only rung four times before Dennis Parish rolled over in bed and answered the screeching instrument. Early morning calls were definitely out of the ordinary, but he didn't expect any major surprises.

"Dennis, its Reilly Reid."

"What do you want at this ungodly hour?" growled Parish.

"I'm down at the Common, and there is a band of what looks like Arabian gypsies down here."

"Reilly, what have you been drinking?" Parish was unimpressed.

"Nothing—honest, Sarge! There's a ship off the Point, and a hundred people are staring at me. Will you please just bloody get down here? Hurry, will you! I don't know what to do with them!" Reilly was trembling with adrenaline.

Dennis hung up, only to have the phone screech again. "What is it now, Reilly? Do you want to tell me it's some kind of practical joke?"

"Dennis, it's Woody. There's a ship anchored off Nepean Island, and it wasn't there last night. Looks to me like they're unloading people! You better get down here."

Sergeant Parish rang his two constables, repeated the information, and demanded their presence at Kingston immediately.

A lone man climbed out of his four-wheel drive. He seemed hesitant as he walked across the field toward them.

"Ah...G'day!" Reilly called out to them. Norfolkers were polite if nothing else. "Are you all right?" Reilly was hesitant, unsure what to say or do. "Is everyone OK?" He was scratching his head. "Is there a problem with the boat?" Reilly waited for a response but got none. "We sure don't get many surprise guests like this."

His eyes scanned the crowd for some sense of comprehension. Did they understand what he was saying? He had been babbling a bit, shock still apparent.

Abbud stepped forward. "We are seeking asylum. Please tell us who we need to report to?"

"For real?" Reilly had heard about 'boat people' but had never expected to meet any. "Geez, Sergeant Parish is gonna love this!"

In the distance, Reilly could see the lights on top of the police car as it snaked its way down Rooty Hill Road. Sergeant Parish had driven down via Queen Elizabeth Lookout to check the horizon for boats. He hadn't really expected to see any.

In the distance, the vessel was silhouetted by the breaking dawn. Sergeant Parish was perturbed when he saw the vessel that Woody and Reilly had described.

Woody called the local chief minister, Harrison Paul, after he spoke to Dennis Parish. Harrison also thought it was some kind of April Fools' Day prank. He strolled to the front parlour of the cottage to look out his window.

Harrison Paul was stunned to see people illuminated by the headlights of Reilly's vehicle. There were dozens of them!

He picked up the phone to alert the locals. This was going to be a day to remember.

The phone network ran red hot for the next fifteen minutes. The locals had enjoyed a mobile phone service only since 2007. Today they would be grateful for it. They were quick to respond to the news, and within minutes, there was a sudden procession of vehicles heading down to Kingston. They came via Taylors Rd, Country Road, and Rooty Hill Road.

Half the local population were on hand at the Common. Dawn had cracked the sky, and in the light of day, the locals, scratching their heads, were inspecting the guests.

Customs officials arrived along with members of the Council of Nine. Norfolk had long been self-governed.

There was a lot of disbelief. Some scratched their heads, others cussed. Most rubbed their eyes, unsure of what was real in the half light of early morning.

What were they to do with them?

"Dennis!" It was Reilly. "Look!" Reilly was pointing toward Philip Island.

Another ship was dropping anchor alongside the *Dragoon*, with a third just coming into view around Point Hunter. They had been so busy scratching their heads that no one had noticed the approach of more vessels.

"Oh, shit!" Dennis Parish stood stunned. "What the bloody hell is going on?"

The *Sento* had sailed into view and anchored about three hundred metres from the *Dragoon*. The decks were filled with human cargo.

While those onshore stared dumbfounded at the sight of the second boat, they were gobsmacked to see yet another vessel round Point Hunter.

The *Batik* dropped anchor just off the headland near Lone Pine. Another hundred-plus souls were onboard. The decks were strewn with people waving to the locals and to the refugees onboard the first two vessels.

Reilly was directed to the end of the golf course. He took his megaphone from the back of his vehicle and stood with it in his hand. "Stay on the boat!" he called to them. "We will come and get you."

He was concerned that they had not understood his instructions when a young man dived into the water on the other side of the *Batik*.

Reilly was horrified to see the young man surface at the back of the vessel with what looked like a small body in his arms. "Oh, no!" Reilly was really upset by what he now saw.

The limp little figure was hauled up onto the *Batik*, where it was quickly wrapped in a shroud. The diver climbed back onboard. Reilly watched as women appeared to be openly weeping, their heads hung low. He was glad he was unable to hear their sobs over the sound of the waves.

Sergeant Parish organised for the cargo boats to be launched from the pier. They had to collect the people off the schooners, and this would take some time. He didn't want anyone else in the water; it was just too dangerous for people to attempt to swim ashore over the rock ledge.

The local entourage towed whaleboats down to the Kingston pier and hauled them into the water. The crane lifted each whaleboat over the deflated dinghy and launched it into the early morning swell. Then the little dinghy was pulled out for repairs.

It took another four hours to unload the human cargo from the three vessels anchored offshore. Tourist minibuses were called to collect the guests from the Common. They were to be taken to the community hall initially.

The first count showed a staggering 357 arrivals from the three vessels that were anchored in Sydney Bay.

"We need to register names, ages, nationalities, etc." Dennis Parish had taken charge while the locals tried to figure out where to start with this sudden intrusion. "Then we need to get them fed and get them to the hospital to check them out."

"I've already notified the hospital," Constable Colleen Norris told her boss. "Doc Edwards is calling in her team. They will be ready when the first bus unloads this lot. Doc will check them for the usual hazards—lice, worms, Hep A, Hep B, smallpox, and anything else she can think of. Then she will make sure they all bathe."

"Who's organising clean clothes? God knows they need some. They stink!" Dennis asked, glad it was all coming together.

"Olive Graham will see to that. She is calling the Country Women's Association as well as the ladies of the Rotary Club. Her first thought was to finally use all the items from the lost-and-found lockers - all those things left behind by tourists over the years. She said she's sick of looking at them," replied Colleen.

"My crew are on standby to feed them." Owen Murdoch was the manager of the local bowling club. "But it will have to be vegetarian because we don't have any halal meat."

"Why would we want that?" Colleen asked.

"Because they are Muslims. They need their food blessed," Owen told her, surprised she had not known.

"After what they've been through, I would have thought they'd be glad to get a feed." Colleen shook her head.

"Well, we don't have enough veggies on the island to feed a couple of hundred vegetarians for days on end, so somebody had better find a cleric among that lot," snarled Sergeant Parish, pointing to the new arrivals. "Then call Bob the Butcher. We need to get some cattle blessed and slaughtered, or this lot will eat us out of house and home."

"OK, boss, I'm onto it." Constable Warren Matthews was the latest police recruit to come to the island. "The supermarket might have some frozen halal meat. I'll check that as well." At just twenty-nine years old, he already had eight years policing experience with the Australian Federal Police, but this was his first month on Norfolk.

Minibuses started to arrive, parking alongside the Common. Archie stepped down from the third vehicle and walked up to Reilly. "Well, they told me at the tour office that I was picking up refugees but I didn't believe them. This is incredible!"

"Yeah, I know. Who'd have thought we'd be dealing with boat people?" Reilly replied. "It's a bloody long way to come!"

"Yep, I can't wait to see how the townsfolk deal with this lot." Archie pointed in the direction of the newcomers. "I think there's going to be some culture shock – especially with all those men wearing dresses!"

"Where are we going to put them all?" Reilly was still scratching his head.

Colleen chimed into the conversation. "Olive will coordinate that. We've got a few motel beds empty this week, so we will start with them." Colleen was in good form. "Has anyone called the mainland to tell them we need help?"

"Yes, I woke the premier, who woke the prime minister," advised Harrison Paul. "The bad news is that today's flight has been cancelled due to the cyclonic winds between here and Brisbane. They will get some stuff out to us on the next plane from Sydney."

"We are going to need a lot of stuff—food, medicines, clothes; who knows what else! We've got tourists coming in tomorrow, so we can't use the motel beds for long. I'm told they will also send some Immigration staff to assist." Harrison was still in shock, but functioning.

"That gives them a couple of days to figure out how to process these new arrivals." The chief minister was stumped. "They should have an update for us tomorrow. Believe me; they are just as surprised as we are. Border patrols do not watch the ocean this far out, so they had no idea these boats were coming our way. Anyway, while they figure out what to do next, we are on our own."

3

ADJUSTMENT

Radio Norfolk tried frantically to keep up with broadcasts all morning. It felt like a constant stream of updates and requests.

Each household on the island was asked to volunteer to billet a refugee family. They were asked to nominate the number of spare beds they had available.

The phones at the community hall hadn't stopped. Dozens of locals buzzed around like Australian blowflies, something rarely seen on Norfolk. The call went out for assistance with beds, blankets, clothes, and food stocks.

Olive Graham had done an amazing job at rallying the troops, allocating refugee families to beds, and ensuring there was food in pantries and other resources where they were needed. She had not worked this hard in years. Olive was exhausted and ready for a beer, and it was only ten o'clock in the morning.

Assigning refugees to local households resulted in a parade of assorted vehicles streaming into the carpark at the community hall. Locals collected their allocated newcomers as though they were picking up goods from the weekly market. It was a busy morning.

For the locals, it was a bit of fun really, sort of like taking school kids on an overnight camp-out. Of course, some locals refused to have anything to do with the new arrivals. The usual fears came out to play. Some people were biased, some just ignorant—a pretty balanced reaction for any community, really.

Fern Morrison stepped up to the Registration desk, awaiting her allocation of refugees. "I can take four," she advised.

As the local potter, Fern had bought a quiet little farmlet on the northeastern side of the island. It was the perfect spot for the laid back existence she needed to feed her creativity. At just 27 years of age, Fern was fiercely independent and had lived alone since returning to the island 5 years ago. She was a reminder of the 'flower children' of the 1970s, with her long hair in dreadlocks. Her paisley patterned dress was covered in streaky mud from throwing pots on the wheel in her studio on the farm. She was always barefoot.

"Oh, that's great" Olive Graham thanked her as she ran her finger down the long list in front of her. She stopped when she came to what she was looking for. "Family number 39 is a family of 2 adults and 2 small children – would that be OK?"

"Sure – that's fine – just point them out and we'll be on our way." Fern was a little nervous.

Olive called to a young man among the refugees. She had been surprised at how many spoke English. "Would you take this lady to the family with the number 39 badges please?"

As they disappeared into the crowd, the next resident stepped forward, and the process was repeated throughout the morning.

As the newcomers settled into households, there was a lot of amusement at different customs, from both sides. Each was glad that meals were to be taken in town. It saved the locals wondering what food to prepare. The refugees were glad to meet up with their friends and relatives at the bowling club. This would be the routine until some halal food could be organised and distributed to each household. Then the refugees could cook for themselves.

Robert Bullock, known as Bob the Butcher, had arranged two large steers to be brought in from the Angus herd. A cleric had been located among the newcomers and the blessings made over the animals. Bob followed the instructions of the cleric and the halal butcher they had with them to ensure everything happened according to their custom.

Some hours later, the slaughtered meat, processed and carved, was delivered to the bowling club. Owen's team went to work; they knew how to throw a good barbecue. They also had some overly large fridges to store the butchered carcasses while the fires were prepared.

The chief minister offered up his spare bedroom to Abbud and his small family. After showing them the facilities, Harrison Paul hoped to get some information from the leader of the group.

"Abbud," he began, "can I ask, where have you come from?"

"From Indonesia, but before that, we came from Iraq." Abbud was cautious about sharing his history.

"Can I ask why you didn't just get on a plane to Australia? Wouldn't that have been easier?" Harrison queried.

"We never got the opportunity. Our homeland has been a warzone for years. It has been in constant turmoil for such a long time that our children have never known peace. Our people have been deprived of work, food, medical supplies and education. Things you might take for granted.

"There was little work to earn money to feed our families. We sold what belongings we owned to get some money together to leave the country.

"We are all tired of war, and just want to give our children a better life – and an education. At home the schools are bombed and we all live in fear. Our children get sick and often go untreated. It is no way to live. We could not go on that way any longer.

"Then when we tried to leave, our government would not give us passports, so we couldn't get visas. Some tried, but couldn't get onto a plane without proving they had a return ticket. It meant we didn't have the choice to come by plane." There was a look of despair from Abbud. "We had some money but few options."

"Then why did you sail around Papua New Guinea to come here?" It was hard for the chief minister to understand their thinking.

"Well," Abbud began, "we were told that we would be turned back if we entered Australian waters by boat. We had seen news reports about Australia turning back boatloads of refugees who entered Australian waters from Indonesia. But we were told that if we landed here, we would not be sent to a refugee camp because this is part of Australia."

"But, Abbud," said Harrison, "this is NOT Australia. This is what they call an external territory. It is far more complicated than you think. Even Australians need a passport to come here. Technically, we belong to Australia, but you have not landed IN Australia."

The colour drained from Abbud's face. His honey-coloured skin was suddenly grey. "Then what will happen to us?"

"Well," said Harrison, "we will do what we can to help you, but it is up to the Australian government to decide."

"But you say this is NOT Australia so why do they get to decide – I don't understand." Abbud was growing agitated.

"Yes, I know - it's complicated, but an external territory is not the same thing as being a state of Australia. There are different laws that apply here. They allowed the Pitcairners to settle on the island so they have the final say on what happens on Norfolk. They are sending their teams in on a military plane tomorrow. I'm afraid I won't know what their plan is until then."

"But if we are not in Australia, why can't we just stay here on the island with you? Can't you make that happen?" Abbud was growing more concerned.

Whaleboats had returned to the anchored vessels. Locals confiscated several hands of bananas thought to have been harvested in New Guinea. For the local fish life, it was an unexpected picnic. All fresh food aboard was seized and dumped overboard into Sydney Bay.

There could be no risk of the locally farmed Norfolk produce being infected by imported diseases. As a result, no fresh fruit or vegetables were ever allowed to be brought into Norfolk from any country—not even from mainland Australia.

While that was happening, the pastoral community was busy in other ways. Across the island, the locals were adapting to a new reality—a house full of people. The motels and apartments that were normally rented out to tourists had been quickly filled. It was suddenly a full house on Norfolk.

The newcomers were able to find their way around easily. All roads led to town. Burnt Pine Township endured a constant stream of refugees walking in to meet kinfolk at the community hall.

It was really odd for the locals to have so many foreigners in town. They were used to seeing Australians and New Zealanders, who were regular visitors. Even the odd cruise ship brought Americans, Italians, Japanese, and the occasional French New Caledonian. *But folk from the Middle East?* That was new.

"I can't get used to seeing all these hijabs and long black robes walking around town," Maggie Christian told the shopkeeper in the shoe store.

"Yes, I know what you mean. It feels like we are in Indonesia or somewhere more exotic than downtown Norfolk," the cashier agreed."

The cultural dress of the womenfolk had felt intimidating to some of the locals who had not previously seen the hijab.

Refugees were found wandering into every store in town. All were polite and respectful. Mothers eyed new shoes and jewellery. Fathers leered at electronic equipment. Children ogled at the toys. All they could do for now was admire these things and hope that one day they would have local money to spend on a few luxuries.

In the meantime, they all loved the freedom of being able to walk around at leisure—for many it was the first time in years. Some of the small children had not known anything but war or months at sea. Now, they played on the grass and sat on the swings in the playground near the hall.

A soccer ball was delivered to the oval behind the hall. It didn't take long for the men and boys to start a game. There was laughter in the air, along with some very strange words of a mother tongue the locals did not know.

At Fern's farm, the father of family group 39 was picking apples in the orchard behind the house yard. He was happily lifting his children into the air, one at a time, to allow them to pick their own fruit. The little ones greedily scoffed the fresh fruit - juice dripping down their chins. It was such a luxury to have fresh food.

Inside the farmhouse, their mother was shown the two small bedrooms that would become their first real home in years. She had not allowed herself to dream of a real bed, or a safe home with birds singing in the trees around them. Norfolk was proving to be idyllic.

"What do you call this?" she asked Fern, pointing to the quilt that was spread over the double bed.

"We call it a doona. Do you not have them at home?" Fern queried.

"Mostly we just had a few blankets to share with the children. Nothing as soft as this" the young mother replied as her hand reached out to stroke the soft layers of the quilt.

Over at the stables, a young refugee male was helping the stable-hands with the horses. As he left the paddock, he asked "Shall I lock the stables?"

"Nah, nobody locks anything on Norfolk" his companion answered

Across from the Hundred Acre Wood was a rather large homestead. Built in the typical 'Queenslander' style, it was elevated with lots of windows to catch the breeze across the valley. Family Group 14 had been invited to stay and were now settling in. The teenage boy was in the paddock watching the cows. His little sister sat on the sofa in the lounge room patting the ginger tabby cat.

"What do I call you and your husband?" her mother, Layla, asked her hostess, as they bonded over a cup of tea at the kitchen table.

"You can call me Helen" replied her hostess, "and my husband is known as Tiger."

"I do not know this name." Layla noted.

Helen laughed. "No I guess you wouldn't. Our surname is Woods, so the locals call my husband after the famous golfer."

"I do not understand." Layla was now confused.

"That's OK, just call him Max. He probably won't answer to his real name, but that's what it is." Helen would have an uphill battle explaining nicknames to her houseguest.

The scene was repeated in many forms in homes across the island. Given the events of the early morning and the disruption to local life, this was a quick and happy transition.

4

FRUSTRATION

"This is Norfolk TV Station One. Here is the news.

"Norfolk witnessed its largest arrival of tourists today, with some three hundred refugees arriving at Kingston. If you have been hiding under a bush, you might not know that we had three boats arrive into Sydney Bay in the early hours of this morning.

"Everyone has done an amazing job at settling in the newcomers, who have all now been housed.

"Chief Minister Harrison Paul has been in contact with the mainland to seek their assistance and directions. Please stand by—we are about to cross to a press conference with the Australian prime minister."

There was a frenzy of journalistic activity on mainland Australia. The news had just broken of the first arrivals on Norfolk.

'*Norfolk Invasion*' screamed the daily paper in Sydney.

'*Refugee Resort*' was the headline in Brisbane.

Melbourne's take on it was '*Norfolk's Nomads*'.

Australians generally thought it was either 'totally outrageous' or 'a bit of a giggle' that the refugees had chosen Norfolk of all places.

Politicians were heard asking one another in hushed tones, "Where's Norfolk?" This tiny external territory of Australia was often overlooked. At just eight kilometres by five, it was easy to do.

Most Aussies knew it was in the Pacific but often got it mixed up with another small island. Lord Howe Island was a neighbour of Norfolk but six hundred kilometres closer to the mainland and a good deal farther south.

Prime Minister William Stephenson was seen on every news channel. He was known for his compassion for those who were genuinely seeking asylum from persecution. As foreign minister for the past seven years, he knew the struggles of those who feared imprisonment, torture, or even murder in their homeland.

Many others saw it differently.

Stephenson had a hard sell ahead of him. "Those who have landed on Norfolk Island are not the first refugees asking for our help. Australia has suffered an influx of asylum seekers in the last decade, as have other countries around the world. The numbers climb when conflicts abroad are at their worst. This is a normal trend that we have seen before."

He was more forceful now. "The 2012 United Nations Refugee Guidelines clearly explain: 'Every person has the right to seek asylum from persecution and serious harm. Seeking asylum is not an unlawful act. Asylum seekers may be forced by their circumstances, to arrive without a visa. They may not be in a position to comply with legal formalities for entry into a country.'

Stephenson explained: "When we signed the international law called the Refugee Convention, Australia agreed to offer these people refuge."

He continued. "The first refugees actually arrived in Australia in the 1930s. They were escaping Nazi Germany. European refugees followed them, with almost a quarter of a million being settled in the years after World War II. These people are now a genuinely accepted part of our community.

"After the 1950s, all was quiet for many years for two reasons. Australia agreed to a set number of migrants who would apply to immigrate each year; then we dictated who could immigrate by developing the White Australia policy. This was a blatant attempt to refine the Australian bloodlines and culture to include only people of English descent."

Stephenson drew a breath. "After years of conflict during the Vietnam War, the boat people started to arrive in Australia in the seventies. Some Indochinese followed them in the late eighties.

"Then, just before the year 2000, people from the Middle East started arriving. These were a little different, though, because they had already travelled as far as Indonesia.

"The problem is that Indonesia hasn't signed the Refugee Convention; therefore, there is no obligation for the Indonesians to protect refugees. As a result, any asylum seeker arriving into Indonesia still lives in fear. They must find a way to move on, and they often find themselves forced to employ 'people smugglers' to get them into other countries, including Australia."

Stephenson knew this was going to be difficult to deliver to the hoi polloi. "After a decade of the persistent annual influx of asylum seekers, Australians had some conflicting opinions about the boat people. While some saw them for what they were—asylum seekers arriving by boat without a valid visa—others saw them as 'illegals', a position engendered by lack of knowledge, lack of empathy, and a media-fed attitude of fear."

The prime minister paused for effect. "These asylum seekers have done nothing illegal. They are NOT 'illegal immigrants'. Refugees are not required to come directly from territories where their life or freedom was threatened. So please, let's show them some compassion. They are a small percentage of the migration of a hundred and ninety thousand migrants that we accept annually. There is a much bigger picture here. We will still continue to take refugees from overseas processing stations, as well as professional applicants and extended family applications.

"Australia will do the right thing by these people. We have found in the past that over ninety percent of arrivals are legitimate when assessed against our Migration Act. It just takes time for us to conduct the appropriate investigations."

Stephenson now had to deliver the politically incorrect part of the message. "Refugees were paying thousands of dollars to buy unsafe boats for the voyage into Australian waters. Sadly, many died at sea. Parliament made a decision to protect refugees from 'people smugglers'. Australia's Border Protection Group locating boats in international waters heading for Australia, will now turn the boats around and send them back into Indonesian waters. We will do this simply to stop Indonesians profiteering from selling boats.

"For those boats that do arrive in our external territories, we now have legislation that requires these refugees to be processed offshore.

"As a result, those who landed on Norfolk will be sent to Manus Island in Papua New Guinea. This is no different to anyone who landed in our other territories, whether Christmas Island or Ashmore Reef."

The prime minister now delivered the line he most hated. "I will take questions."

Pandemonium broke out among the journalists. Some were in uproar that 'detention centres' would again be used. Others just hated Stephenson and would do anything to show him up. It was called political fodder.

"Prime Minister, aren't they just jumping the queue?" barked the reporter from the *Sun Herald*.

Stephenson responded, "There is no 'queue'. Anyone seeking asylum must first leave their home country. Some flee by land, others by plane, some by boat. Most are so poor that they only get as far as their neighbouring country, where they are processed through refugee camps. That's why we also accept our share of refugees from camps. So the only effect on numbers is the overall number we can take from refugee camps. That number is decreased if we take more people arriving by boats. Next question?"

"Prime Minister, is it true that there are more than three hundred arrived on Norfolk?" This time it was the Northern Territory reporter. "I've been to Norfolk Island, so I know they don't have a lot of spare resources. How will the locals cope until our teams can evacuate the refugees?"

"Yes, there are over three hundred people. We are organising food, clothing, and emergency supplies. This is the same as we did last week to help in Noumea after the cyclone. It will take another day to coordinate. Defence Force planes will leave here late tomorrow to fly these supplies over to Norfolk. They will also take Immigration personnel to supervise the interview process." Stephenson was getting bored. "These planes will then be used to transport the refugees to Manus Island over the coming days.

"I'll hand over now to the minister for defence for details." Stephenson was glad to be able to step away.

Harrison Paul had taken a phone call just ten minutes before the news bulletin. He had not been surprised to hear Prime Minister Stephenson tell him the refugees were to be moved to Manus. Harrison did not know how the refugees would take the news.

Abbud watched the press conference in silence. Alongside him, the chief minister scrutinized Abbud, waiting for a reaction. Harrison watched the refugee swallow hard as the news was delivered, but Abbud said nothing.

Abbud needed to breathe fresh air—he was choking with fear. They had not anticipated this. Their dreams were being dashed – all hope was lost. But how could they go back to Iraq? Nothing had changed in their homeland – war, destruction, despair. Abbud needed to speak with Fadi and the others.

"Would you excuse me, please? I need some air," Abbud apologised as he rose to leave the room.

Harrison called Margaret Christian, the one who was on the Council of Nine. There were two other

Margaret Christians on Norfolk. One was known as Meg; another was nicknamed Peggy. This one was Maggie. As head of the legislative assembly, she was the first to be told of the decision.

"Maggie, have you heard? They're going to send them to Manus." Harrison was matter of fact.

"Well I can understand that, Harrison," said Maggie, unaware her words were being over-heard. "Manus is horrible. The living conditions are appalling from what I've seen on TV. Even the refugees hate it so much they are rioting. They even have rats crawling over their beds at night, if reports are accurate."

"Yes it doesn't look good, by all accounts" Harrison responded. "That riot last week was pretty desperate wasn't it?"

"It's not good when there are deaths in custody." Maggie answered. "And can someone tell me, why does it take two years to process them on Manus? I don't think that's healthy for anyone's psyche, especially for the children." Maggie was appalled at the prospect of anyone living in those conditions. "Then after years of waiting most of them are sent home anyway – what's the world coming to?"

Behind her, the refugee house guest, Nidal, stood in the darkness outside the back door, absorbing the description of life on Manus Island. It was a horror story he did not want to hear.

"Yes" Harrison agreed. "I think it would be better if the Defence Department allowed them to stay on Norfolk. We could probably absorb them into the community - we could certainly use some more permanent residents at the moment. They might bring another dimension to the place—you know, a different cuisine and so on. It might wake the place up a bit. But, it's out of our hands, unfortunately." Harrison was back in his role as chief minister. "The law is the law."

Fadi met with Abbud at the oval. He had brought with him the captains and deputies from the other two boats.

"We have a problem," announced Abbud. "It seems we have been misled. We will not be allowed to stay here on Norfolk. Instead, we are to be sent to a refugee camp at a place called Manus Island."

"That can't be right," argued Ilias, captain of the last boat to arrive. "We were assured we would be processed here and allowed to stay. Why send us to another island—why not leave us on this one?"

There was an angry unison of voices behind him.

"Well, it gets worse," Nidal broke in to the babble of voices. "I overhead them talking about Manus Island. It's a horror camp. People are dying before they are processed. They keep them there for two years with rats climbing over them. My children are not going to live like that – they have been through enough already. And my wife would kill herself before being sent somewhere like that." His anger was rising now, desperation in his voice. "Then they said people are sent back to their homeland anyway. I can't do it – I can't tell my family they have to go back to where we came from."

"I can't see that the Australian government would send us to somewhere like that" Abbud declared.

"Oh, really? Just like our government would never let us down? Well, we all know how that turned out." Nidal was vehement in his distrust of governments – his past history had left a bad taste in his mouth when it came to the authorities.

"What would you have me do?" asked Abbud.

"The others will be here by tonight." Hassan was the handsome captain of the *Sento*, the ship that had followed *Dragoon* into Sydney Bay. "That will cause more chaos. The locals barely coped with us arriving today. They will never cope with the others coming in."

"So we will outnumber the locals." Nidal declared. "Why don't we just take over the island? Put the locals to sea, and we can stay," he half joked.

They turned to look at Nidal, smiles growing on previously stressed faces.

"Well, it's tempting, but how are you going to make that happen?" It was Abbud's turn to smile.

"We can work something out. There aren't that many locals," Nidal encouraged the group. "None of us want to go to Manus, and we know we can't go home."

"The Australian government gave Norfolk to the Pitcairners," Hassan interrupted, "so why can't they give it to us?"

"We will have a trading card – we have to take the locals and tourists as hostages until we can negotiate to keep the island for ourselves." Nidal commanded.

Fadi interjected "No, you can't do that."

"We have no choice." Nidal glowered at him. "Do you want to go home – back to war and terror for your family? No, there is no other way."

The others agreed with him. They could not keep running. This was the best chance they were going to have for freedom.

It quickly became apparent that they must first stop the planes from landing on Norfolk. That way, the Immigration officials could not start processing refugees for Manus Island.

Destroying an airport without being discovered would not be easy. They had no bomb-making equipment with them nor the skills to make bombs. These were pacifists who had fled their homeland to escape violence. They had no desire to resort to it here.

Survival, however, was another thing. They were not prepared to be shipped off Norfolk.

"Sayyid, what do you think?" Ilias queried.

"We walked past a road plant on the way into town. There are big mechanical diggers we could use to tear up the tarmac across the runways. That would stop the planes from landing. Then they can't fly us out." There was a cheeky sneer from Sayyid.

"Yes, that's a good first step," Hassan suggested. "Then we would need to knock out their communications. There is only one station transmitting both TV and radio, I'm told, and then just communication from the airport. That should be easy enough."

"No, you are wrong. There is another communication hub out of town, near a place they call Anson Bay. We need to find it and take it out as well," Ilias said.

"How are you going to cover the noise of all this demolition and destruction?" Abbud challenged.

"From what I have seen," Nidal explained, "the airport is fairly isolated from the local houses. That helps to reduce the distance the noise could be heard," he said, hoping this to be true.

"Well, I don't know about that, but the generators being used in town are so damned loud, the locals might think the noise was from there. They don't normally use generators. I'm told they have only brought them out to power up the extra resources needed for us, so they are learning to ignore the noise."

"All right, say that both those things are true. By the time we start rounding up locals, there won't be many who can hear the noise anyway. So we just have to target the homes around the airport to start with. Does that make sense?" Abbud was a born leader.

"Yes, that makes sense," Nidal replied. "By the time we head up that hill to the communication towers, the area should be pretty well cleared of locals."

"But what about the rest of the locals? They are spread out across the island. We would have to round them up and bring them into the hall," Ilias said.

"That's the whole idea." Nidal laughed at him then. "We leave the tourists until morning and just concentrate on rounding up the locals tonight.

"It may take us a day or two, but once we have it under control, we can use the radio on the *Kris* to contact the Australian government to begin negotiations."

Dennis Parish was exhausted after such a dramatic start to the day. It felt as if he had run all day. He was glad to be locking up the small police station. Night was looming, and it was time to head home.

Locks are generally not used on Norfolk, but he was compelled to lock the station. Each police officer had a gun that was kept in a locked gun cabinet in the back of the building. There were also a few rifles on hand in case they were called on to put down an injured animal.

There was little crime on the island—some petty theft occasionally, but not much else. Sometimes one of the locals had too much to drink, though they were rarely rowdy enough to warrant arrest. There was a murder once, some years ago, and that had ignited concern across the local community. A bloke from New Zealand had later been arrested and convicted. Then a chief minister had met an untimely death at the hands of his son. These events were rare intrusions into an otherwise peaceful existence.

Policing generally consisted of checking that car registrations were up to date. Sometimes they even checked car speeds in the thirty-kilometre-an-hour school zone. The speed limit around the island was fifty kilometres an hour, but Burnt Pine and Kingston were both forty-kilometre zones. Hard to imagine, but the police actually set up radar speed traps around the island. The locals were renowned for ignoring the speed limits. Tourists were better behaved in cars.

Island life was a step back in time to days long forgotten in the big smoke on the mainland. Here they trusted their neighbours, respected other people's property, and waved to one another as they passed in cars.

As the sergeant slid the key into the lock, the phone began to chime. Dennis's shoulders sagged with weariness. "Bloody hell!" he whispered under his breath. "Will this day never end!"

He walked back to the reception counter and picked up the wall phone. "Sergeant Parish," he answered.

"Sarge, it's Muzza." Murray Christian was the airport manager. "I'm up at Mount Pitt—came up to check the radar beacons at the lookout. Mate, you're not going to believe this."

"Try me," laughed Dennis. "After today, I would believe just about anything, I think!"

"Well, I'm looking north over Bird Rock, and I can see more boats coming. I'd say they will be at Cascade Pier within the hour. I just counted eight of them."

Sergeant Parish dropped the phone.

5

MORE BOATS

The news bulletin had already begun when the calls went out once again to the locals. The weary could not decide whether to leave the latest boats to anchor at Cascade Bay until tomorrow or try to collect their occupants tonight.

Vince Fletcher Hawkins, a senior member of the Council of Nine, was of the opinion that they could wait until tomorrow.

Adam Fletcher and Maggie Christian disagreed.

"The cyclone's still circling between Norfolk and the mainland—it could change direction at any time," Adam said. "If that happens, these new boats could be smashed against the rocks. We just can't risk loss of life."

"I agree with Adam. We have no choice," Maggie insisted. "They have to be brought ashore tonight. It is the humane thing to do, and we can't risk them jumping into the water. Having that little boy die this morning was bad enough."

"Here we go again." Vince shook his head. "Then we better call Dusty for help."

Kevin 'Dusty' Street was the local fire brigade chief, and he also managed the island's road maintenance plant. He was asked to bring the fire engine down to Cascade Bay, to light the area with spotlights from the truck.

Dusty could bring a small diesel-powered generator for the spotlights. This would allow them to operate the crane under lights. They needed to safely lift speedboats and fishing boats into the water from the concrete jetty.

There was no room on the roadside along the jetty to park other large vehicles that had powerful headlights. Besides, their batteries would run flat within the hour, and this would be a long night.

The call went out to the regional fire fighters and volunteers asking them to assist. The local fishing fleet was called in to launch their vessels into the now-calm waters of Cascade Bay. The whole operation was underway within forty minutes of Dennis Parish dropping the phone.

In the last light of day, seven fishing boats with powerful engines were on their way out to the refugee vessels approaching from the north. Fishing boats had large, heavy-duty spotlights to enable them to land their catch nets—these were employed tonight to light their way to the approaching Indonesian schooners carrying refugees.

Each captain of an incoming vessel was advised to anchor at least five hundred metres from his closest neighbour. As each vessel anchored, the captains were directed to organise their occupants into groups to be transported back to the pier. In the area adjacent to Cascade Waterfall right across to Simons Water, the sea was littered with vessels.

Boat engines could be heard zooming across the moonlit bay toward the refugee schooners. The engines were quiet only long enough for the boats to be loaded with refugees.

Women, children, elderly, young males, teenagers, babies. The fishing boats were loaded and unloaded, then loaded again. Refugees descended from schooners across the bay. They just kept coming—hundreds of them.

The calmer seas allowed them to use the fishing fleet this time. It made the whole process easier and faster. But they kept coming; there seemed no end to the number of refugees on these vessels.

Cascade Pier overflowed with people and vehicles. The carpark around the old rusted whaling-oil vat was clogged with tourist buses. Mini buses had again been called into play, to ferry passengers into town.

Weary locals manned the pier to direct newcomers to vehicles. Serena Hollowes, a nursing sister, was on hand to isolate those refugees who needed to be taken to the hospital for attention.

A constant stream of vehicles arrived down Harpers Road from the west and Cascade Road from the south. There was a traffic jam where the two roads intersected a couple of hundred metres from the bay where the pier was situated.

There was little room to negotiate large vehicles. The road was a series of turns that wound down toward Cascade pier. It had never been designed for a large amount of heavy vehicle traffic—or even this number of mini buses running a shuttle back to the town oval. It was chaos!

Vehicles ran out of fuel; nobody could remember driving this number of kilometres in a single day before. The call went out to the three local petrol station operators to fill oil drums with fuel to deliver to stranded vehicles.

Fishing boats also ran dry. The petrol deliveries now changed to diesel for the boats to continue their shuttle service. There would be a very large fuel bill to be settled tomorrow. Everyone hoped the Australian government would pick up the tab.

The hospital had long given up trying to process refugees tonight. They had already been overwhelmed today. All staff had been called in from rest days and other leave to work an extra shift today. They were all exhausted. On top of this, they had each taken in refugees from this morning's count.

Doc Edmonds called the chief minister. "Harrison, we are going to have to put them on the oval tonight. There is no way we can process them. I can only handle any that need immediate medical care."

Chief Minister Harrison Paul agreed with Dr Helena Edmonds. The locals were directed to move the latest arrivals onto the oval behind the community hall. The hall was to be used only for the young and the frail. Tables would be set up inside to assist with food and clothing.

Otherwise, everybody else would be camping out. At least at this time of the year, the temperature was still a pleasant twenty-three degrees Celsius overnight. The only concern was the likelihood of rain and strong winds. If the cyclone once again changed direction, the refugees would have to be taken inside under shelter. All three local clubs and all of the local restaurants would be used for shelter if needed. Club managers and restaurant owners were advised. This was the council's plan B.

The landing operation took nearly ten hours. Tahu Waneka, a New Zealand native who had lived on Norfolk for nearly forty years, was the owner of the local tour buses. He drove his last vehicle home at 2.45 a.m.

The final count tonight was another 938 refugees. Added to this morning's arrivals, this brought the total number to 1,395 arrivals today.

This was more than the current permanent population of Norfolk.

The TV station had not become aware of the latest influx of boats until after the news bulletin had finished. The station personnel had gone home to bed before knowing the final count of refugees from the new schooners that had arrived in Cascade Bay.

Most locals missed the news broadcast and the prime minister's address because they were down at Cascade Bay bringing more refugees ashore.

When the final count was known, Harrison Paul tried to call the mainland. His phone would not dial out. He tried his mobile. Nothing.

6

RAIDERS

The township was quiet. All the activity was down at the pier. The locals who were not involved at the pier were at home. They were occupied settling in this morning's arrivals.

Women from two different cultures got to know one another over the eternal cup of tea that connects women across the world. Refugee menfolk made their excuses to walk into town. They said they wanted to pay homage to Allah as a group. Little prayer mats were tucked under their arms.

More generators were brought in to light the oval—they were as noisy as the refugees with their conversations in a foreign tongue.

As the new refugees were delivered to the oval, it was impossible for the locals to keep track of the numbers on hand. They didn't notice groups of refugee males slip away into the darkness beyond.

In bushland behind the Lions Club playground, a meeting of the refugee males took place. They were outside the range of the headlights that pulled into the carpark at the hall.

While the rescue operation was underway at Cascade pier, the group led by Abbud was taking action.

"By midnight, we will have enough of our own people to take charge." Abbud liked the plan.

Groups were organised and areas assigned. Men headed off in different directions depending on their mission.

The road plant was just out of town. Its gates were held closed with a large chain and a single padlock. The men climbed over the fence. Ilias, captain of the *Batik*, commandeered the Kubota excavator—its key had been left in the ignition in typical Norfolk style.

Ilias drove it straight through the closed gates, which buckled under the weight of the vehicle. The tractor-like road digger was slow, so getting to the airport would take time. It lumbered along the dark road behind town.

As he approached the fencing around the airport perimeter, Ilias accelerated the motorised monster and let the vehicle smash through the airport fence onto the grassy field.

He was careful to avoid the diesel storage tanks on the side of the runway. They would need the contents later.

Farther along the fence line, the terminal buildings were deserted at this hour. The little fire brigade building could be seen close by.

In the paddock opposite the terminal sat a one-hundred-year-old bodhi tree—one of only two on the island. This one was massive, covering a whole quarter acre. Its dense foliage would provide a possible hiding spot if Ilias needed one.

The aerial towers for the radar were in the open field. The digger headed toward them first. Ilias smiled as he thrust the digger toward the aerials. Metal latticework crumbled beneath the weight of the vehicle.

The aerials were pancake flat by the time he had finished rolling the digger back and forth.

The runways were positioned along different compass directions—north/south and east/west. Prevailing winds dictated which of the runways would be used on any given day, according to the predominant conditions at the time. On approach, aircraft were advised by Norfolk Air Control of the best runway to use.

Ilias identified the intersection of the two tarmacs as the best place to cause major disruption.

As he allowed the motor to idle, Ilias could hear the hum of the generators at the oval in the distance. The muffled noise of the digger was also camouflaged by the voices he heard coming from the oval. With over a thousand people down there, it sounded like a rave party in progress.

Beyond the airport, on the side roads, there were very few locals at home to listen for odd noises. Everything about today was odd. No one seemed to take any notice of the mechanised hum at the airport. Ilias watched around him to see if anyone came running. Nobody had.

Opposite the airport, on the area along Ferny Road, the buildings were inhabited by local businesses. Tonight, these were quiet.

Ilias allowed the digger to roar back to life. He put it to work gouging the centre point of the intersecting tarmacs. It was his intention to carve a metre-wide channel across both runways. Any plane's wheel that hit a ditch that wide would suffer significant damage. Ilias allowed the digger to wreak havoc on the tarmac. It took nearly three hours to complete the disruption, but it was enough to cause an aircraft to abort landing.

A pilot might not see the scar on the tarmac in time, so Ilias left the digger parked alongside the ditch. From the height of a cockpit, a pilot could see the yellow mechanised monster from several kilometres away. Ilias wanted to stop the planes—he did not want to crash them. He meant no harm.

It was Qadim, the captain of the *Kris*, who had been given responsibility for destroying the communication base outside town. He chose a group of raiders and headed out toward Anson Bay. The map had given up the location of the repeater station. This was the island's link to landline phones and the Internet via underwater cable to the mainland.

The project, known as SPIN, had been completed in 2010, connecting eleven Pacific nations to high-speed broadband. Norfolk shared the undersea cable connection with Samoa, New Caledonia, and French Polynesia, among others.

The main cable nestled on the sea floor about 180 kilometres south of Norfolk. From there, the spur-line cable ran back to Anson Bay, on Norfolk's east coast. Here, the telecommunications facility was used as the landing station for the cable. These buildings housed key nodes that were necessary to deliver broadband to the community.

The updated fibre-optic cable replaced the old satellite system. Locals now enjoyed high-speed con-nections. It was a vast improvement on the previous 512-kilobyte download rate and 256-kilobyte upload speed.

Norfolk Hospital had benefitted from new tele-medicine access to specialists on the mainland. The Central School suddenly found they were able to con-nect to remote one-on-one learning opportunities and vocational education. Local businesses got access to Internet-based tourism information and bookings. E-commerce flourished.

Qadim was about to take all that away again.

Once he had located the telecommunications fa-cility, he realised he needed some large equipment to make an impact. Across the road, a farmhouse supplied the answer.

"There has to be something we can use over at that farm," Qadim told his men. "Let's go look."

Watching for any movement in the area, they slipped across the road.

They stepped over the rungs of the cattle grid and then stayed on the grass along the driveway. Their footsteps would not be heard from the farmhouse if they stayed on the grass verge. The gravel driveway would have crunched loudly underfoot if they had used it.

The front door was unlocked, and Qadim and his men entered the farmhouse. "Find the bedrooms," Qadim whispered to his men.

In the first bedroom, they found a family of refugees sleeping. Qadim roused the man by holding his hand over the man's mouth. Eyes were instantly alert and staring into the dark. Qadim leant forward and whispered into his ear, "Get up quietly. We need your help."

The man sat up and pulled his pants on. He stood to follow Qadim into the hallway. He knew why they were there—to subdue the owners of the farm.

"You two, in there." Qadim pointed to a bedroom with two single beds and a couple of children sleeping. "Don't wake them until I give you the signal that we have the adults under control."

Hearing loud snoring, he moved along the hallway toward the back of the house. Qadim was surprised to find it was the woman who was snoring so noisily. *Geez, that's bad,* he thought as he shook his head. *Your poor husband!* He placed his fingers around her nostrils, forcing her to open her mouth. She snorted in automatic response.

Her husband woke at the sudden noise from his wife—he was clearly well attuned to her nighttime breathing habits. He rolled over to look in her direction and was confronted by the sight of Qadim standing over her. He sat bolt upright so quickly that his head was spinning as the blood in his veins tried to regain equilibrium. He was unaware of another man in the room.

Qadim's companion put a hand over the husband's mouth and wrapped his arms around him from behind. The husband tried to spin toward the source of the restraint but was pinned firmly in place. The hand had slipped from his mouth to confine his arms.

"Jesus, what are you doing? Don't you touch her!" he yelled at Qadim and his companion.

"We are not here to harm you, but we are going to take you hostage." Qadim tried to make his voice calm and comforting. The edict was to avoid violence if at all possible.

"What do you mean, take me hostage? What the hell's going on?" The husband was frightened more by that statement than he had been by the sight of a man standing over his wife.

The wife was now alert, and she yelped as she re-alised there were men in her bedroom beside her husband. Qadim glowered down at her and raised a finger to his lips to warn her to stay silent. She pulled the sheets up over her head and started to sob.

"Your family will be taken into town. You will be safe if you don't struggle and don't try to fight us. Otherwise, I cannot guarantee your safety or that of your wife and children." Qadim looked menacingly at the husband now, determined to get the message across.

He called to the others in the children's bedroom next door. "Wake them and put them in the car. One of you can drive them back to the school."

"The school? Why the school? What are you people playing at?" The husband was getting more anxious and started to squirm.

Qadim's companion used the man's belt to restrain his arms behind his back while they moved him to the car. The wife's hands were tied in front of her with her own neck scarf. She left a trail of urine on the floor as she was led up the hallway. Qadim understood she was nervous and frightened beyond belief.

The men were gentle with the children, having woken them by talking to them until they opened their eyes. The noise from the adults in the next room had hastened the process. The children were asked to dress and were led to the car unrestrained. They took some toys and books with them as well as their pillows and blankets.

The remaining members of the little refugee family were awake now and standing in the doorway to their bedroom. They witnessed the procession of people up the hallway. As the farmer's wife passed them, she stared into the eyes of the Iraqi woman, who simply whispered, "I'm sorry."

When the family had left, Qadim set his men back to the task at hand. "Yes! Grab what you can. Keys should be in the vehicles. We can use both of those tractors and that little truck. Let's move it!"

A couple of tractors and a flattop one-tonne truck were located in the house yard near the roadway.

Qadim directed three of his team to seize the vehicles and take them to the telecom site. There, they set about wreaking havoc.

The flattop truck was driven straight through the main doors of the facility. It turned right along the corridor, smashing walls down as it went. The driver located the main electronic switchboard and quickly flattened it. Any electronic node that was housed in that room was rendered inoperative.

Outbuildings were decimated in turn, tractors easily crashing through soft external walls. Apart from some large cement blocks that were used as foundations, it was unheard of on the island to build with bricks. Builders had utilised timber products and some lightweight imported Colourbond-style siding materials for external walls. These yielded under the mass of large tractors weighing several tonnes.

In the far northeast corner of the telecom yard stood a single large satellite dish. It did not stand a chance against two tractors and a flattop truck. Once toppled off its base, the dish crumbled under the vehicles' repeated attacks.

Nidal, second in command on the *Sento*, followed Qadim out the gates of the Road Maintenance Depot. He was driving the Caterpillar earthmover. The tractor-like vehicle, fitted with a front-end loader bucket, proved to be a powerful beast. The access along Grassy Road would take the earthmover to the island's highest lookout.

At 327 metres above sea level, Mount Pitt was almost the highest point on the island. Nearby Mount Bates exceeded it by just 1 metre, but it was inaccessible to road traffic.

The road up to Mount Pitt was steep and winding, with several hairpin bends. There was only moonlight shining onto the road to light his way.

Nidal could not risk headlights being seen from Cascade Bay or anywhere else across the island. He did not want his intentions discovered until the job was complete. The vehicle was heavy and awkward to negotiate along the narrow road, so his progress was slow.

From the top of Mount Pitt, the view was spectacular. In the distance, Nidal could see the lights from the fishing fleet. They zigzagged across the water to the newly arrived boats to carry human cargo back to the pier.

Nidal could see the lights of Kingston and his own vessel in the distance. It was less than twenty-four hours ago that they had rounded that point near Lone Pine.

Dozens of houses were lit up across the island. He knew many would now be empty, their lights left on when the occupants were removed unexpectedly.

When he finally reached the top carpark, Nidal turned the tractor up toward the crown of the hill.

At the top, he drove it through the metal barrier that protected the island's communication towers, and then he moved the loader to the high side of the beacons. Gravity would help topple the weight downhill. Then he nudged the loader up against the first beacon.

As he engaged the gears to propel the loader forward, the beacon began to creak against the pressure. Nidal pressed on the accelerator. Nudging harder against the base of the structure, he managed to topple the first radar beacon. Sparks flew as electric wires were ripped apart. The structure landed with a thud on the ground beyond.

Nidal backed the tractor up far enough to turn it around. Then he propelled it forward once more until it banged into the base of the second beacon. It separated from its foundations. Again and again he reversed and thrust the tractor forward until the beacon gave up its position. It finally crashed to the ground.

Lastly, Nidal turned his attention to the remaining aerial tower sitting atop Mount Pitt. As the front-end loader pushed into the metal tower, the teeth caught on the frame. The loader shook like a dog with a bone, swishing left and right, until it dislodged the twisted aerial. The metal frame tumbled through the thick bush surrounding the summit.

He had destroyed the final remnants of electronic communication with the island. There would be no more contact with planes, no more radio transmissions, no more TV broadcasts.

Nidal did not realise he had knocked out the mobile phone network as well.

Fadi left the oval with his assigned group of refugee males. They crossed the distance behind the bowling club out of sight of the local officials who were taking details at the hall. When they located the car-hire business on New Cascade Road, Fadi explored the building before smashing a side window to gain entry. Reaching through the broken glass, he turned the door handle.

There were still a dozen hire vehicles sitting idle in the parking lot. They were waiting for tourists who had not arrived.

In typical Norfolk style, the keys were not hidden in a safe—they were on display on a keyboard in the reception area. On a plaque beneath the keyboard, the vehicle registration numbers were marked to pair keys to vehicles.

Fadi handed out keys to the waiting group. The men took the vehicles and started moving them out along the back roads around the island, spreading out to all points.

They would deliver a group of their own men to each farmhouse and homestead. These men would take over the land holding, round up the locals, and deliver them to the school.

The school would be used as the new isolation camp. There were kitchens and bathrooms and classrooms that could be used to house locals. Small groups of locals would be easier to manage in separate classrooms. There was a perimeter fence at the school that would be easy to patrol.

There was a rifle range to the north of Anson Bay that would yield rifles and pistols. These might encourage the locals to submit to the refugees' plans.

They could thank the local tourist map for all the information they needed to implement their plans. Everything was so conveniently marked on the maps, which were available at every restaurant and business in town. The tourist information centre in front of the hall had plenty of these maps—they had been given out to every one of the new arrivals.

Abbud would stay at the oval, where he would continue to liaise with the new arrivals. He needed to send more men out along the country roads to take over farms. The island was small enough for them to walk to a hundred homes within a kilometre of the township. Groups of men wandered off into the night.

Those with cars headed out to the northernmost corner of the island. Fisherman's Lane was the farthest point from the activity at the pier. It was quiet and dark along the island's lonely country lanes.

Fern Morrison, the local artist and potter, was in her workshop at the back of her property. She had new pieces that must go into the kiln tonight.

After a busy day helping in town, she had brought home a young family of refugees. The wife and toddlers had gone to bed early. The young man had gone back into town to worship with his countrymen.

Just past the intersection of Anson Bay Road and Fisherman's Road, Fern's house sat about twenty metres back from the roadside. It was uncommon to have cars moving around this area at night—there were only five homes past hers on the way to the cliffs that marked this edge of the island.

When Fern heard a car turn into her driveway, she assumed it was the young father returning. She left the workshop to greet him but was blinded by the headlights coming down the driveway.

The car parked near the fruit trees that lined the drive. Car doors opened, and three stout males, dressed in robes, stepped out into the night garden. Fern was instantly uncomfortable—she sensed something was not quite right.

The young father approached her, but her eyes were now on the others with him. Her arms were suddenly wrenched behind her back.

She bellowed in pain. "What are you doing?"

They said nothing as they ushered her into the car, squeezing her in to the backseat of the Hyundai along with two other men.

The five homes past hers had already been emptied.

Along from Fisherman's Lane in the area of Bullocks Hut Road, the locals had built a road out to the Captain Cook Monument. This memorial was built on the northern side of the island to commemorate Cook's landing on Norfolk.

It didn't matter that he hadn't landed at this particular spot; it made a nice place for a memorial. Cook was believed to have landed a bit farther along the coast at Anson Bay. Here in the north, overlooking Cathedral Rock and Elephant Island, the tourists got some great photos and could picnic under shady trees.

This area housed about thirty families along with a lovely little restaurant that served a great Devonshire tea. The houses were separated by acres of farmland and forest. Few could even see their neighbours' lights.

Distance solved most things, and any noise from next door was muffled by the trees and paddocks between the family homes.

Each home was systematically taken over in turn until the area was emptied of locals. Intimidation was all that was needed; violence was avoided, though it had been used as a threat.

Cars filled with abducted locals moved unnoticed along the back roads. Refugees ferried locals back to the school. From the northern end of the island, they could avoid the township by using Anson Bay Road, going down past the maze and St Barnabas Chapel, and then taking Headstone Road. From there, they circled the airport and then moved onto New Farm Road, down past the Hundred Acres and through the picturesque avenue of Moreton Bay figs.

Cresting the hillock, they followed this road down onto Country Road and back up Taylors Road. From this end of Burnt Pine Township, it was just a short distance along Queen Elizabeth Drive into the school.

Norfolk Central School was situated just around the corner from where Middlegate Road melds into Cascade Road.

The refugee raiders had completely skirted the activity at Cascade Bay. They had been unseen by the vehicles carrying new arrivals back into Burnt Pine Township.

Locals had gone back to school for the first time in years.

Another seven vehicles snuck out of town to the area of Stockyard Rd on the eastern side of Norfolk. Between Martins Road and Two Chimneys Road were another sixty homes, mostly farmlets isolated by acreage. The housing was denser in the village around Hibiscus Drive.

One by one, these farms were emptied and the occupants moved back to Middlegate Road. The school buildings started to fill. Fifty refugee males stood guard with rifles at their sides. The perimeter fence was well guarded.

In the headmaster's office, there was an old bunch of keys—each marked with the name of the building block followed by the classroom number. Classrooms were filling fast. Locals were scared and exhausted from the day's activities.

Maggie Christian was bundled into a car with her five-year-old granddaughter, Abby, and driven to the school. The pair had been frog-marched into the staff room, where the other members of the legislative assembly had been deposited during the evening. They had been joined by some of the more prominent locals.

When the guard closed the staff room door, Adam Fletcher nodded at Maggie as he approached her. Adam, at thirty-two years old, was little more than half Maggie's age. "You OK, old girl?" He tried to sound lighthearted to ease the tension, especially around the little girl.

"You can cut the 'old girl' comments, thank you," Maggie responded, now brave enough to be cheeky again. "What the hell are we going to do?"

"None of us has figured that out yet, Maggie. I think we should just get everyone settled and try to figure out the rest in the morning." Adam was being optimistic.

"But they have us under lock and key. Have you seen the armed guards?" Maggie was getting angry. "To think we let these people into our homes and welcomed them with open arms. God, it makes my blood boil. The bloody hide of them."

Adam frowned as he motioned toward the little girl holding Maggie's hand. "Let's just keep calm. No point trying to figure it out tonight. We are all overwhelmed and exhausted from today's events. This isn't the time to put the thinking caps on; we can brainstorm in the morning."

"Yes, I suppose you're right," Maggie conceded.

Being tired and terrified was not the best time to come up with a workable plan. No one had been harmed so far, so there was no immediate concern for their safety. *Best to wait until morning and assess their situation in the light of day.*

Maggie settled the little one onto the floor—she had been allowed to bring the little girl's bedding with them. She lay down beside her granddaughter and began to sing to her.

As she started to drift off to sleep, Maggie's last thought for the day was that tomorrow would come soon enough.

The refugee raiders had ignored tourists in motels and apartments across the island. There were so few tourists on Norfolk this week that they represented no immediate threat to the refugees. Tourist accommodations came in all shapes and sizes and were well spread out across the island. From ritzy motel rooms to self-catering cabins, every taste was catered to on Norfolk.

Abbud knew his people had filled most of the tourist beds. They could assess the remainder in the morning.

From the oval, the groups of refugee males had quietly moved out of town. After scouring the farthest areas of the island, they had returned to the huddle outside the hall. Fresh groups had taken their places, maps in hand. They located farmhouses and homes, rounding up locals from the middle of the island. The last area to be searched was around the base of the national park on the town side of Palm Glen.

Farmhands from the stables were collected along with others from a couple of dairies closer to town. Horses sensed intruders as the refugee males entered the property. The sound of whickering from the animals brought their handlers outside to investigate. "Who's there?" the stable boy had called into the night.

"It'll just be the dog from next door," his mate had answered him.

They were stunned when they were confronted by five males encircling them.

"Oh, shit," the stable boy said, gulping in disbelief as they were bundled into a waiting car.

Selwyn Pine Road to the north and Mission Road to the west were scoured for any homes that might be hidden down dirt lanes, and there were a few. Homes were located, and their occupants were subdued, bundled into vehicles, and delivered to the refugees guarding the school.

With most of the outskirts of town now cleared of locals, the refugees concentrated on the area closer to town. There was still the local soft drink bottler and the houses within the township, as well as those homes out along the road to Cascade Bay. These were all scouted in turn. The residents were cornered and forced into vehicles for the drive to the school.

At the bottom of Grassy Road sat the Norfolk Hospital. In the early hours of the morning, the wards were quiet, except for some snoring. As the nurses' feet clip-clopped through the halls, a group of men pushed through the front doors. Patients were rudely woken and bundled into waiting buses.

The nurses, fearful of the sudden intrusion, were quickly compliant. They were made to help with the last two patients in the end ward. Essential bedding was pushed into waiting vans, and medications were gathered on the way out. Within fifteen minutes, the hospital had been emptied.

There were now 380 refugee males guarding the school. They were outnumbered by locals at a ratio of nearly three to one. The influencing factor was that the refugees were armed.

Most were armed with lengths of timber, some with tools taken from garden sheds; others had bows and arrows taken from the archery club. There were a handful of rifles and pistols, and three police revolvers. These had been taken from Sergeant Parish and his constables when they returned to the police station at 2.40 a.m.

The last local was rounded up and delivered to the school at 3.45 a.m.—an hour after the last refugee had been transported to the oval.

The last person rounded up was Woody. He had been operating the crane down at Cascade pier. Woody bid

Tahu goodnight as the last minibus drove away, then waved off the last of the fishing boats as trailers left the pier. Woody walked back to his Toyota Corolla, climbed wearily behind the wheel, and drove up Cascade Road.

He was blinded by headlights at the top of the first hill, where he was stopped by a roadblock. An arm reached in through his open driver's window, turned off the ignition, and opened the door. Woody was unceremoniously yanked from his seat and bundled into the back of a station wagon.

He was not going to make it into his own bed tonight.

The first tourists strolled toward the café a little before 7.00 a.m. They were surprised that it was not already open for early coffee and breakfast. The Peppertree had the best coffee in town and was usually open from 6.00 a.m. Half a dozen tourists waited on the grass verge of the village strip.

"God, I'm hanging for that coffee," Ida complained to her husband.

Along at the roundabout, the other favourite café-cum-bakery also stood silent. There were no tempting aromas wafting from the kitchen, no steam from the coffee machine. In fact, there were no cars parked in the driveway and no staff walking around inside.

"Where is everybody this morning?" Gerry asked his breakfast partner.

Tourists stood around scratching their heads, wondering where everyone had gone. The town was eerily quiet.

The tourists were rounded up shortly after seven in the morning. They too were escorted to the school. This was a holiday that would not easily be forgotten.

All were being fed and had ample facilities for washing and other ablutions. They had been taken in groups for a half hour's exercise during daylight hours. There were a lot of groups to be rotated throughout the day. The school playground had never been so constantly busy.

As the day progressed, the locals and tourists became resigned to their new reality. They were given blankets and pillows but would have to sleep on hard floors.

Tensions eased, and Abbud was able to finally reduce the number of guards at the school. They had to stay alert and keep on the move, constantly patrolling the grounds.

Abbud's teams had taken all day to record numbers as they brought the locals and tourists to heel. Once he had that information, Abbud had to decide how to proceed. He did not want the locals to stay on the island. He would put them to sea on the refugees' own boats.

He had learnt that the natives were descendants of the *Bounty*, so they should know how to sail a vessel away from Norfolk. Noumea was only a few hundred kilometres away.

They will have radios to call for help if they need it, he admitted. There were radios on both the *Java* and the *Kris*. They had only been able to afford two radios, having spent all their money buying the boats.

The *Kris* had been delayed off Papua New Guinea when it took on water and had to be repaired. Otherwise, it would have been the lead boat arriving into Kingston. Instead, it had arrived at Cascade Bay with the second group of refugees.

Abbud started to think about their new home. The island was big enough to easily sustain over five thousand refugees. He realised they had found the perfect homeland for their new lives. Here they could farm the land, grow their own vegetables, and establish the life they had always dreamed of.

Tomorrow he would send a message to their friends in Iraq. They had suffered long enough. Now that he owned the island, they could send for their families and friends.

He would use the radios on the boats that had arrived last night.

7

ARCHIE

At eighty-eight years of age, Archie Jackson had seen it all. Nothing much surprised him these days. He had arrived on this earth twelve years before the outbreak of World War II. Archie had watched his father go to war, again. Two older brothers also served, though both lads had lied about their age to enlist.

Archie had a tough childhood. Mum had nine kids, with six still at home when war broke out. There were few luxuries; most days there wasn't even enough food for everyone, so Mum often went hungry. New clothes were unheard of—Archie grew up in hand-me-downs. There was no underwear until you were a grown man, and shoes did not make it onto his feet until he finished high school. Thankfully they lived in a warm climate, so cold weather was rarely a problem.

Archie was the oldest child at home during those years. He was the man of the house before he was even a teenager. Driving a tractor, milking cows, growing vegetables—all became part of his everyday life. He learnt to be self-reliant.

His younger siblings looked up to him. It was up to Archie to teach them how to farm the land and help around the house.

Even clearing the land was Archie's responsibility while his dad was away. He took it all in his stride—there were few choices. You just got on with it and did what you needed to do.

Archie had some vivid memories of his childhood. He had once scared the local vicar with an ill-timed explosion of dynamite. The horse-drawn cart the vicar used to get around the island was often seen around town. It was unexpected in Archie's part of the island.

When an old pine tree fell across the track to town, the only solution to move the large tree was to blow it up. Archie did not have the tools to cut it up, nor did he have the wherewithal to spend three days trying to cut through this vast girth of pine.

So, just as his dad had shown him, Archie located some old dynamite from the barn. Dad had some left over from blasting the road down to the old farmhouse. Archie placed it inside a knothole along the middle of the fallen tree. With match in hand, he quickly struck the match against the flint, ignited the wick, and ran for cover.

It was only then that he heard the approaching cart and realised it was the vicar. By the time Archie found the voice to yell a warning to the approaching visitor, the explosion had rung out across the farm.

The vicar's horse bolted, with the vicar holding on for dear life. Archie knew the vicar was praying, because he could hear "Holy Jesus" being called to the skies. The horse and cart disappeared round the bend in the track at a mighty quick pace. In fact, the old nag could have won the crown at Royal Ascot! Archie had no idea a horse could move that quickly.

It was some days later before Archie found out that the horse had run clear across the island. The vicar had managed to pull the old nag up just before it got to the cliffs. The poor vicar had thought someone was shooting a canon at him.

Archie never did tell his mum!

Then there was the time he was chopping wood for the old stove. As the axe came down on the chopping block, his younger brother reached out for the kindling that was about to be split off.

Archie was devastated to see the tip of the kid's pointer finger land on the chopping block. He bundled his sibling into his arms and stemmed the blood flow with his shirt. Archie raced the youngster back to the homestead, where his mother met his screams with a panicked look.

They patched the poor kid up, but his hand was never the same again. He couldn't count to ten because he only had nine and a half fingers! The kid never blamed Archie, but Archie blamed himself.

After the war years, his father and brothers came back to the farm. They brought stories of the war with them, along with a ham radio that they had built from leftover parts discarded by the navy. The men had put them to good use—they had managed to put them together into a working radio.

They would sit around the radio at night, talking to other ham operators all over the world. It became a nightly ritual that served as a source of fun and friendship. It also meant they had emergency communication in times of trouble.

"Dad," Archie asked, "why do they call it a ham radio? What's it got to do with a pig?"

Old Man Jackson laughed. "Nothing at all, son. I think they called it amateur radio, so the 'am' became 'ham,' and it just stuck."

Archie adored his father, even though the old man had a nasty temper. He soon learnt to avoid his dad if the old man was cranky. As he grew up, Archie realised how much he had learnt from his old man. He had even learnt Morse code to use on the ham radio.

Then there were the life skills the old man had taught him. As a result, Archie knew his way around the toolshed and could build most anything that was needed. He had even built a small cottage on the top paddock when he married Irene at just nineteen years of age.

The pair had been inseparable until she passed away nearly three years ago—a lifetime spent together before she became ill.

They had just celebrated their sixtieth wedding anniversary with a wonderful little party in town arranged by their granddaughter, Serena. Surprisingly, there was a lovely letter of congratulations from the governor general of Australia and another from Her Majesty the Queen. Such a wonderful day together—the last of his special memories of his beloved wife.

Six weeks later Irene was gone, and life would never be the same again.

Serena comforted him as best she could. She was still getting over her own grief. Poor girl had lost both her parents in the earthquake that hit Christchurch in 2011.

Archie's daughter and her husband had been visiting his family back in NZ. That day, they were in the local TV station to give an interview to promote Norfolk tourism. The quake that devastated Christchurch brought down the entire building that was the TV station. Archie lost his daughter that day; Serena lost her mum and dad. Many others also died that day. Christchurch had never fully recovered; neither had Archie or Irene or Serena.

It affected Irene badly, and Archie believed she just gave up after that. Serena had been left orphaned, and Archie and Irene had taken over her welfare. She was a young adult but unsure of herself in the world. She needed a support system; she needed the parents who were no longer there.

At twenty-three years old, Serena was in Sydney finishing her nursing degree when her parents died. While she loved the people on the mainland, the noise and the smells made her yearn for home on Norfolk.

Of course, she was influenced by the fact that her childhood sweetheart was still on the island, with no plans to leave. Adam had made it clear he wanted to marry her and raise a family on Norfolk. Serena came home when she graduated and had been nursing at the Norfolk Hospital ever since.

Over the years, the welfare scenario changed. Years after they had Serena move in, it was now Serena who was caring for Archie. Ever since Irene had passed, the tables were turned. Now his granddaughter looked out for him.

Archie still lived in the little cottage he had built for his beloved bride. The homestead had been sold off years ago, but he had managed to buy the land where the cottage sat. There had been only one child raised in the little cottage. Like her mother, she was now gone. The cottage was as sad as Archie.

Serena lived just up the road with her fiancé, Adam Fletcher. She still managed to visit Archie every day, often arriving with a meal or a cake. His favourite was her home-baked chocky slice; he could eat that every day.

The old ham radio was still in the back shed—his man cave established long ago. Some days he had just needed to escape the womenfolk, much as he loved them.

Airwaves still connected him to his mates around the globe, though not as often as they used to. It helped with the loneliness that had pervaded his days since Irene passed.

He was a sociable man who liked nothing more than a good chat. Locals called him Have-a-Chat Jackson. That was the nickname that appeared in the local phone book against his landline number.

Archie could spend his days just telling old jokes. They were told and retold dozens of times a week. His 'dad humour' was legendary. There were only a few on the island who did not already know the punch line to any of Archie's jokes.

He was an interesting character. Full of life despite his years, Archie was active and healthy. He had a wicked sense of humour, and his mind was still sharp; he figured out crosswords almost every day. He was widely read and had even learnt how to send e-mails. He knew how to search the Internet and used the computer most days, even though it still frustrated him.

When you were a child of the 1920s, you had grown up with the Toaster Principle. You just wanted to plug it in, turn it on, and know it would work. He hated that these new tech tools had to be loaded with programmes like Word and Outlook, or needed 'apps' downloaded. *You can have that!* he thought.

He was a bit of a hoarder—you never knew when you might need a thing. So the house and shed were full of things. It proved a useful habit when he had to repair any old gadget that suddenly went kaput. Archie could rustle up a spare part or engineer one if he had too.

Without the ability to do that, his old ham radio would have been defunct a long time ago. What would he do without it? He had even fluked a link with an astronaut back in the 1980s—now, that was a story. He was trying to get hold of his old mate in Launceston and got the astronaut instead. They had a good chat, and Archie told him all about Norfolk. The astronaut had trouble seeing it in the middle of the Pacific, but Archie assured him it was there! Just a speck, but it was there.

Archie couldn't see the Sputnik, either, but without it being almost overhead, the conversation could not have taken place. Pity he'd forgotten how to pronounce that bloke's name, but he couldn't spell it either.

He found out later that it was fairly common for astronauts to carry amateur radios with them, even on space shuttle missions. They could have conversations by holding their VHF FM radios to the window and talking to schoolchildren when classrooms were directly beneath them.

Sometimes Archie was just happy to listen to other conversations on his radio receiver. He could troll through the frequencies until he found something interesting. He would turn the dial anywhere above the AM radio band. Some nights there was nothing until he got into the citizens band. Daylight was better for long-distance conversations in those short-wave frequency ranges. Higher frequencies meant shorter wavelengths.

Mostly as a ham operator, he would use the FM repeater from the local radio or TV station these days. Conversations could be transmitted much farther that way. Amateur radio satellites still offered a new option as well. When the satellite was overhead, it acted as a repeater, allowing uplink and downlink simultaneously.

Sometimes, of course, voice transmissions couldn't get through, but Morse code signals could because they worked on a series of beeps. Archie didn't understand all the new technology, but he still managed to keep using his old ham system in most situations, with or without new inventions. Ham radio operations didn't even stop during natural disasters, even though phone systems were usually disrupted.

Even during last week's cyclone in New Caledonia, Archie still got a message from a little Frenchman he knew up there.

Shame he hadn't told Archie that the boat people were coming his way.

Today was Archie's afternoon off work. He had helped to transport the refugees from Kingston up to Burnt Pine and to the hospital this morning and then headed home. He had not known about the second fleet of refugees that had arrived this evening. In fact, Archie wasn't even aware of the existence of the second group of boats. He'd been nowhere near the phone when it rang.

When the news came on the TV, Archie was asleep in a hammock in the lower paddock underneath two apple trees. While most of the locals had gone down to Cascade Bay this evening, Archie was snoring, blissfully unaware of the added excitement as the day drew to an end.

The group of raiders who had come down Rooty Hill Road had found no one at home at Archie's little cottage. They had not seen him in the shadow of the trees in the lower orchard. They hadn't heard his snoring either, so his existence went unnoticed.

Even Serena had not reported his absence when she was rounded up and taken to the school. She had wrongly assumed he was part of the group driving the newcomers up to the hall. She hadn't been worried about him; she had just assumed he was elsewhere.

Just after one in the morning, Archie woke up. He stretched and then eased himself out of the hammock. He wandered back to the cottage. The old wooden boards creaked as Archie stepped onto the back porch. He walked past Irene's favourite chair, opened the back door, and turned on the kitchen light as he stepped inside.

There was a note from Serena; she had been there just before five in the afternoon. "Beef casserole in fridge for your dinner—Enjoy. On nightshift, so please call me before you go to bed. Love, Serena."

Her shift would not finish until 3.30 a.m., so she would still be at work. Archie picked up the phone and dialled the number for the hospital. Nothing. He tapped the cradle, jiggling the little button up and down. There was no dial tone. Archie frowned.

In the bedroom, he found his mobile phone and scrolled the contact list for Serena's number. He pushed the call button and waited for it to start dialling. Nothing. He tried dialling again. Nothing.

What the hell? Archie was bewildered. He plugged the charger into the wall plug and turned on the power point. The phone confirmed it was already fully charged. *Hmm, that's weird. Guess I'll have to try again later,* he said to himself.

Having slept in the orchard for hours, he was now wide awake. Archie made himself a cup of tea and turned on the TV. Nothing. *Bloody Hell, I give up. Everything's gone on the blink.* He picked up a book from the side table, frustrated that he had missed the evening news bulletin.

He was still in the armchair when he woke up at 8.30 a.m. Archie did not remember finishing his tea nor putting his book down. Age had its downside. Falling asleep came too easily these days.

After another cup of tea and some Vegemite toast, he tried the phone again. *Still no dial tone.* He cussed. The mobile phone didn't work either. Serena would be home asleep after her night shift, but Adam might be around. He could walk up the road to find out if Adam knew why the phones weren't working.

Three hundred yards was just a pleasant stroll for Archie. The morning was warm and mild as autumn snuck in across the island. The sun shone and the birds sang—all was calm along Rooty Hill Road.

Adam and Serena had bought the land at the peak of the hill above Queen Elizabeth Lookout. They had built a little round house across the road from Woody and Megan.

There was a spectacular outlook down across the World Heritage site and out to Philip Island. It was a peaceful spot.

As Archie turned into the property, he saw their cars were all in the driveway.

Adam wasn't at work. *Great—he might be able to get my phones working,* Archie mused. He was growing concerned. *Maybe Adam had dropped her home. She must have had car trouble. Better just check she's OK,* he continued to himself.

He stepped onto the front patio and knocked. There was no answer, so he knocked again in case they were both in bed asleep. There was still no answer, so he opened the unlocked front door and called out, "Serena, love, are you home?"

A brief inspection proved the house was empty. Archie wrote a note and left it on the fridge under a magnetic bottle opener. He was concerned—the cars in the driveway made no sense—but he might as well head home. There was nothing for him here.

8

DEFENCE

"Come in, Air New Zealand Flight 74; this is Defence Force Radio in Brisbane. Please state your emergency."

"This is Air New Zealand Flight 74. Advise unable to land in Norfolk due to heavy vehicle parked on tarmac. Unable to contact Norfolk communications. We must divert to Kaitaia, as we are now low on fuel. We will not make it back to Auckland and are unable to refuel on Norfolk. Over."

"Say again—vehicle on tarmac?" Brisbane was incredulous; it didn't make sense.

"That's right," copilot Emma McCormack confirmed. "Unable to raise Norfolk to get vehicle moved. We have now flown over the airport several times.

Closer inspection shows the tarmac has been dug up. What the hell is going on down there?"

"Thank you, Flight 74. Confirm you are declaring an emergency and are low on fuel. Will advise Kaitaia you are incoming. Please be aware they have a less than ideal runway length for your aircraft. Good luck." Brisbane signed off.

Secure phones screamed at Defence Force bases across several states on mainland Australia.

Prime Minister William Stephenson was informed of developments on Norfolk Island—or what they knew of them, anyway.

The head of Defence Forces, Commander Annabel Bryson, called an emergency summit. Her boss, Defence Minister Laurence Kellerman, called the meeting to order.

"What do we know?" Kellerman asked.

"Only that Norfolk had three hundred refugees arrive yesterday morning," said Annabel Bryson. "And now, today, we have lost communication and have a dysfunctional airport."

"What do we gather from that?" Kellerman demanded.

"We can make a lot of assumptions, sir, but we have had no confirmed communications from the island in the last fifteen hours. Nothing at all!" Bryson was on edge.

"Have we sent air force planes in to take a look?" Kellerman was getting agitated.

"Sir, Norfolk is fourteen hundred kilometres off the mainland. We have a plane on its way there, but we don't expect to learn any more than we already know from the Air New Zealand flight. As you know, it has now diverted to Kaitaia." Annabel was alert to the mood in the room.

"So, what's the plan? What do I tell the prime minister?" Kellerman huffed.

"Sir, we need to ascertain whether the island has been taken over." Bryson was on thin ice, and she knew it.

"Do we really think that's a possibility? After all, how many residents are there and how many refugees? It seems unlikely," Kellerman countered.

"It may seem unlikely," accepted Bryson, "but we believe it is possible. How else do we explain the loss of communications and the destruction of the airport?"

Annabel drew a deep breath. "Sir, until we can re-establish communications, I believe we have to treat this as an act of terrorism."

"How do you suggest we handle it, then, Commander Bryson?" Kellerman frowned at her. He was responsible for her actions when the buck stopped. He also had to explain this to the prime minister.

"Sir," Bryson continued, "HMAS *Fremantle* is already steaming toward Norfolk. They were on assignment in Noumea, cleaning up after the cyclone. Captain Johnson has been advised that the *Fremantle* has now been redeployed. They will arrive in Norfolk in approximately twelve hours' time."

"What do we do in the meantime?" asked Kellerman.

Annabel softened her tone. "We wait, sir."

As the satellite passed over Norfolk Island, it snapped off enough photos to tell a story. The story was becoming clearer by the hour.

"Kellerman," the voice answered as he picked up the phone.

"Sir," Annabel Bryson's voice broke the silence, "we have satellite pictures." She paused. "Firstly, they confirm a large vehicle on the runway and a wide ditch across the tarmac. They also show the peak at Mount Pitt. Both radar beacons are on their side, torn off their structures. Telecommunications are down across the island. The telecom base at Anson Bay has been destroyed. Their satellite has been decimated. This is definitely human intervention, not a natural disaster."

Annabel drew breath before continuing. "More importantly, the pictures show more boats. This time, they have anchored off the north coast of the island. We had previously been informed of three boats arriving yesterday morning. We did not expect any more, yet now we can see eleven boats in total."

Annabel went on. "If they had three hundred refugees on the first three vessels, then they have potentially landed another eight hundred from the other vessels."

"Good Lord, woman. Do you really think they've taken over the island?" Kellerman struggled to take it all in. "I thought they were refugees."

"Sir, the satellite pictures also show a large number of people hanging around the perimeter of the local school." Bryson wondered if her boss would understand the significance of this.

"So?" Kellerman was abrasive.

"Well, any activity would generally be seen in the township, sir," Annabel explained. "There is no visible activity in the village this morning, whereas the school is two kilometres out of town. Plus, it's school holidays." Bryson paused to let her boss soak up the information. "Then there appears to be a contingent of guards around the perimeter. I don't believe these are locals, sir."

"Anything else?" queried Kellerman, scratching his head.

Bryson waited before delivering the final blow. "The guards are carrying weapons, sir."

Kellerman's face drained of colour.

Submarine HMAS *Kendall* had been on joint naval exercises off the Queensland coast. Captain Ewen

McIntosh was surprised to be told to turn his vessel toward Norfolk Island.

Ewen had visited Norfolk many years ago as a teenager. He longingly remembered the lazy summer days spent swimming and snorkelling at Emily Bay. Ewen could not imagine terrorists taking over Norfolk.

Obeying his orders, Ewen turned the sub toward the southeast. He would send a landing party to investigate when they arrived. If memory served him, there was a small beach on the windy side of Cemetery Bay. The beach was large enough for them to put a landing party ashore unnoticed. The adjacent golf course was on land a couple of metres higher than sea level. He remembered making out on the beach, hidden from the view of others. *What was her name?...Alice, I think.* Ewen smiled at the memory.

The beach would give ample cover for their divers to arrive unseen. He would make sure they arrived during the dark hours of night. He would have to surface to let the divers off the submarine. Ewen wanted to make sure no one knew they were there until he decided to let them know otherwise.

It would be quite a hike from there up Rooty Hill Road, toward the school. He would split the teams and send one up Middlegate Road as well. The map, down-loaded from the island's tourist website, had proved useful. It showed a guide hall that could be used as a base. It was a couple of hundred metres from the inter-section of Queen Elizabeth Drive and Cascade Road, near the school.

As expected, the air force jet that flew over Norfolk Island reported the additional boats. The jet had flown high, not wanting to alert the refugees to any military presence.

Powerful lenses were trained on the island. These showed little activity except around the school.

Along with the satellite images, this drew a dis-quieting image for the defence minister back on the mainland.

He immediately called for additional resources to be sent to Norfolk. He wanted the island reclaimed as quickly as possible without loss of life. Kellerman placed another call to the head of Defence Forces, Commander Annabel Bryson.

"HMAS *Adelaide* will leave Brisbane within the hour, and HMAS *Wangaratta* will be four hours behind them. They will be in the waters around Norfolk by midnight," Bryson advised her boss. "Aircraft carrier *Townsville* has been rerouted. She will be within reach of Norfolk before dawn. We can then send her parachutists in under cover of darkness.

"In the meantime, I have asked HMAS *Fremantle* to continue toward Norfolk but to anchor at the fifty-kilometre mark. Until we know more, I don't want their presence to aggravate the situation. They will be out of sight of the island's horizon. We need to have reinforcements in place to start an assault." Bryson was confident in her decisions. "We need more information before we storm the island."

In the corner of the staff room, a group of locals huddled in discussion.

Kevin 'Dusty' Street held their attention. "We have to find a way to get a couple of blokes out of the school. We need to contact the mainland to tell them what's happening."

"How?" demanded Maggie Christian. "Harrison says they've knocked out all communication. Even our mobiles don't work."

"Do we know if the landlines still work? They run through underwater cable, remember. What about e-mails—ditto with them. Can we find a laptop?" Dusty asked the group.

"No Internet," Vince confirmed. "I jumped onto the headmaster's laptop last night. Connection is as dead as a doornail."

"What did we do before mobile phones?" Sergeant Parish wondered aloud. At just thirty-eight, he was part of the generation that found it hard to imagine life without mobiles or computers.

"Shit!" exclaimed Dusty. "Ham radio! We used ham radios over long distance."

"Does anybody still have one on the island?" Vince Fletcher Hawkins remembered the old radio operators and their clunky equipment.

"Buggered if I know." Dusty only had part of the answer. "Let's ask around, discretely. We might get lucky."

Serena Hollowes was using her nursing skills on little Abby Christian. A very large splinter had found its way into the child's thumb.

Maggie watched on, keen to see how her grand-daughter was coping with the extraction process. She cradled Abby until the splinter was safely deposited into a gauze swab. As soon as the disinfectant had been applied, Abby jumped up and ran off to her friends, who were sitting across the room. Her recent tears were long forgotten.

"Thanks, Serena. You're a gem." Maggie was pleased her granddaughter's tears were over.

"How's it going? Any ideas on getting us out of here?" Serena asked calmly.

"We're trying to find someone with an old ham radio. Don't suppose you have one?" Maggie joked.

"No, but Grandpa does." Serena looked her straight in the eye.

A very broad smile broke across Maggie's face. "Does it work?"

"Hell yes. Grandpa would drive us nuts without it." Serena laughed. "When it comes to his ham radio, he's worse than I am with the mobile."

Maggie kissed her and went in search of Woody.

9

RADIOS

By midmorning, the refugees were again meeting to discuss their future. This time, that future was based on staying right there on Norfolk Island.

Abbud needed a megaphone to address such a large crowd. He found one in the hall.

"It is my privilege to tell you we have taken over the island," he announced to a cheering crowd. "Now we must learn how to run it successfully."

Abbud continued, "It is fortunate that we all have good accommodation and food in the cupboard for now. However, we will need groups to manage the farms and the crops that are ready for harvest. We need meat for the table and fresh crops planted, so we have a lot of work ahead of us.

"A team will be needed to run the supermarket and others to supervise the cattle farm and the dairies. Can anyone make cheese? Does anyone know how to pump petrol? How many of you have medical or dental skills to assist in running the hospital? We need teams to cook for the hostages at the school.

"I have appointed each of the boat captains to the task of organising you into trades."

The crowd understood the need to quickly take control of running the island. No community could survive without basic infrastructure and services.

At Norfolk Central School, the locals spent an un-comfortable night. Conditions were cramped; amenities were stretched beyond capacity. There was a smell of human odour starting to linger inside the warm classrooms.

Today there were fewer refugee groups patrolling the grounds. Many of the guards were sleeping under trees in the school playground. Those who had been on patrol during the night were now dismissed. Others took their places.

In hushed tones, the locals discussed their current position. At times, the conversation became heated. Mostly, though, the discussion was sombre. They could not risk being overheard by the guards.

The town councillors had been segregated into the teachers' staff room. The refugees thought it best to remove the decision makers from the general population. It never occurred to them that they were putting all the decision makers together to brainstorm.

"Who's going to go find Archie?" Maggie Christian asked the group of councillors.

"I'll go," offered Woody. "I can check on my farm and vehicles while I'm out there. I'll find Archie, and he can contact the mainland. If I can't find him, then I can have a go at the ham radio myself."

Reilly Reid stuck his hand up. "What are the chances that the refugee boats have workable radios?"

The councillors looked at him. "Bloody hell, why didn't we think of that?" Muzza demanded. The airport manager should have known the boats would use radios.

"I could swim over to find out," Reilly offered. "If I find a radio, I can try to contact the mainland or maybe even a ship at sea. Their radios should work the same as the ones in the ranger station."

"Great!" exclaimed Maggie. "But how do we get you two out of here?"

"Well," said Reilly, "when I was at school, we would sneak out one at a time. We just went to the bathroom in a group of six, but only five came back. It worked every time we had an assembly." He was clearly pleased with himself.

They all laughed at him, but in the end, that was exactly what he did.

Woody, on the other hand, wanted to find the broom closet.

He had spent years working as the handyman around town and a whole summer just fixing things at the school. Woody knew there was a manhole in the floor of the broom cupboard. It was used to access the plumbing underneath the staff rooms. There was room under the building to conceal one adult. From there he could climb out from under the building and scoot across to the pine grove. He could watch and wait until it was safe to make a dash to the tree line next door.

Woody edged his way across the staff quarters. Checking that no guards were watching the narrow corridor, he ducked across the hall and into the broom closet. Underneath the buckets and mops, he found the latch that released the floor trap.

He eased his frame down beneath the floor and pulled the trapdoor closed above him. He had thirty metres of playground to cover before he could escape into the pine grove beyond the fence.

Just five metres away was the shrubbery around the kids' picnic area. Woody checked for prying eyes. When he thought the coast was clear, he darted across the distance to the shrubs and slid underneath the flowering hibiscus into the clumps of ginger plants.

Vince watched from the windows in the staff room. "He could have been a baseball player the way he slid into that plate," he told the others later.

Woody had to crawl among the shrubs to the other side of the picnic area. He made it to within ten metres of the trees in the paddock next door. He was about to move when he heard voices closing in on him.

A group of refugee guards had come over to the picnic grounds for a smoke and a chin-wag. Woody lay frozen to the spot in the bushes near their feet. He listened carefully but understood nothing of what they said. His breathing was shallow so as not to give away his position.

It was nearly twenty minutes and two cigarettes before the refugees went back to their posts. Woody listened intently as their steps subsided into the distance and the refugees rounded the corner of the staff room building. *Go!*

He darted across the remaining distance, keeping his frame low to the ground. Woody hoped it was enough to keep him out of sight. He relied on the shrubbery to camouflage his movements.

Squeezing between the lower rungs of the old wooden fence, he clambered into the shadows of the pine trees. He was out of breath and trembling by the time he stopped deep inside the pine grove. Adrenaline had caught up with him, and his heart was pounding.

He sat for some time before his body recovered enough to move again. Woody stood up and meandered between the rows of trees until he came within sight of the roadway.

Cutters Corn was a little lane that intersected Collins Head Road behind the school. With the lane in sight, Woody waited to make sure he was not being watched. There were few farmhouses around this part of the island, but he had no idea where the other refugees were. They had to be staying in homesteads across the entire island. Woody could not take any chances now. He had to get to Archie.

Reilly snuck around the corner of the toilet block as the others wandered back to the staff room.

The guards looked up as the group approached the door to the building. Because there were a number of people in the group, all talking at once, the guards just assumed the same number were returning. No one had counted them going out nor counted them coming back in. That was what they were relying on!

Reilly waited behind the water tank next to the patch of clumping bamboo. No one had come looking for him, so, three minutes later, he started to inch away from his hiding place.

He was metres from the back of the tennis court, where the kids parked their pushbikes. The racks were empty even though the school was full. Reilly snaked his way past the first bike rack and into the bushes at the end. He ducked behind the flowering shrubbery used to define the teachers' carpark.

A group of guards were loitering around the driveway to Cascade Road. They talked, they laughed, and they smoked. Reilly waited.

As he glanced back at the windows of the staff room kitchen, he saw Maggie watching him. She realised he was cornered, with the guards standing around the driveway. Maggie screamed and screamed.

The guards turned and ran to the staff quarters. Screams had to be investigated. As soon as they turned their backs on him, Reilly ran. He scurried across the driveway and over the road to the grounds of the Uniting Church opposite.

Maggie would later tell him that she had simply reported seeing a mouse to explain her screams. It had the required effect of moving the guards, though they were more than a little miffed by 'a stupid woman and a mouse'.

Around the back of the church, the vicar's car was still parked where he had left it. The vicar was now in residence at the school, along with the other locals. Reilly could not risk taking the car, but he checked that the keys were in the ignition in case he needed it later.

He hopped the fence into the yard behind the church. Staying alert for any sign of human inhabitants, Reilly was careful where he walked. He did not want to arouse suspicion with the sounds of his footfalls.

With no cars in sight and only the PlayCentre Kindergarten overlooking the intersection, Reilly took a chance. He ran across the road into the yard opposite. The little cottages normally occupied by tourists should have been empty.

A noise inside the closest cottage alerted Reilly to take cover. Two children ran out the back door, letting it slam behind them. They threw a ball down the yard, and a small dog chased after it.

Reilly pushed farther into the undergrowth near the buildings. The dog turned, aware of the movement, and started yapping in Reilly's direction. Reilly took a step backward and, in doing so, disturbed a bird's nest. The bird took fright, squawking urgently as it took to the sky.

This seemed to satisfy the dog, who ignored any further noise or scent from the undergrowth, where

Reilly stood frozen to the spot. A rolling ball distracted the dog. Reilly made his move.

He followed the fence line away from the cottages. Another hundred metres farther on, Reilly crossed Middlegate Road, near the guide hall. Up the side of the guides' building, he spotted an old pushbike. The tyres were inflated, the seat in one piece. Reilly climbed aboard; he would test the brakes on his way down the hill.

A number of farmlets had been established along Middlegate Road. Most of these had no direct view of the roadway. Many were built behind high hedges that gave them privacy from passing vehicles headlights. Others were built high but with outlooks over Kingston. Reilly passed underneath the windows, apparently unseen, and then disappeared down the hill toward the World Heritage site.

It was less than two kilometres down to Kingston and across the back of Emily Bay to the golf course. He spun the pushbike past the golf members' clubhouse and onto the first hole. It was hard yards pedalling a pushbike across the grass. Adrenaline kept him going.

Reilly flung the bike to the ground on the slight rise of the course above the little beach at Cemetery

Bay. He scrambled down to the sand below him and started shedding his clothes onto the sand.

His boxer shorts were his only swimming attire. Reilly flung himself into the tepid water and pushed against the current, which tried to propel him back to the beach.

The waves were rough on this side of the coast. High cliffs nearby showed the rough-cut damage of years of heavy waves. Unlike Emily Bay's calm swimming beach, this area was not recommended to swimmers. There was plenty of exposure to the sea along Cemetery Bay, but the actual sandy beach area was not large. Nor was it safe.

Reilly was a strong swimmer. He had grown up in Bondi and spent his teenage years as a volunteer lifeguard. Strong swells did not deter him. Distance swimming was second nature when you lived at the beach. Reilly had competed in several ocean marathons before becoming a park ranger. He was definitely in tune with the world's natural elements.

The *Sento* was anchored about 150 metres off Lone Pine. This meant a swim of nearly a kilometre around the headland from Cemetery Bay Beach. This was still easier than trying to manoeuvre over the rock shelf at

Slaughter Bay and getting cut to shreds on the rocks and coral residue.

Making sure the road was quiet, Woody raced across to the southern side and scrambled up the verge and under the wire fence. It had been over half an hour since he had left the staff room. He had made it less than two hundred metres from the school. Keeping low, he kept scurrying across the open field.

Once he was beyond sight of the road, Woody stood full height and started walking toward his home in search of his neighbour. He took advantage of any protection offered by trees wherever he could. He kept out of sight of the farms he passed on his way toward Rooty Hill Road. No point taking any risks, he thought.

Woody was alert to any sounds around him. He baulked when cows were spooked by something in the distance. He could see a dark-skinned teenager in the next paddock. Woody watched him return to the farmhouse and enter the back door.

Another hundred metres farther on, a little creek started its path across the hills toward its entry point into Emily Bay. Woody followed the creek for a little while before scooting around Muzza's place and then up onto Rooty Hill Road.

From there, he kept to the side of the road, staying alert for the sounds of approaching vehicles or voices close by. Another ten minutes, and he could see Adam and Serena's place, and his own home opposite.

Woody crept across the road and into his back shed, hidden under the choko vine. His truck was still in the shed, and his wife's town car was parked in the driveway. He could hear voices in the yard. Peering through the shed's window, he could see a middle-aged woman talking to his chooks. A young girl was petting them.

He watched them for a while, unsure whether there were others around his property. There appeared to be no other movement in or around the house. Woody decided it was just the woman and her daughter.

The choko vine gave him cover on the way back out to the road. He ran across to the other side of Rooty Hill Road and ducked behind the bougainvillea that strangled Serena's fence line.

Archie's cottage was down the hillside, in the little dale overlooking the creek. Woody eased his way through the apple orchard and past Archie's hammock.

No sign of his mate out there. Woody headed for the cottage.

Reilly took longer than he expected to reach the *Sento*. He had lost form since he last swam a marathon and was pretty well knackered when he finally grabbed hold of the anchor rope.

There was a small ladder strung over the side of the boat. Reilly assumed this was how the refugees had left the vessel yesterday morning. He was thankful the rope ladder had been left behind. It made it easier for him to climb aboard.

He was out of sight of Norfolk, as the boat had swung around in the changing tides. Reilly was boarding the vessel on the side that faced Nepean Island.

There was little structure inside this crude little vessel—just a deck and some basic equipment below deck, but no radio. Reilly found a compass and a GPS system only. He could not believe there was no radio gear. *Shit!*

It didn't take long to turn over the few belongings onboard the *Sento*. Reilly realised he would have to check the other two boats. He dived over the *Sento*'s side and back into the waters of Sydney Bay. He swam overarm toward the next vessel.

The *Batik* was anchored about two hundred metres from the *Sento*. It was slightly smaller but just as sturdy. Reilly pulled his weight out of the water with the aid of the rung ladder and clambered aboard. The smell hit him as he moved below deck to look for radio equipment.

He thought the *Sento* had smelled bad, but this was even worse. *How long were these people on this boat?* he thought as his nose turned up at the smell. He forced himself to stay below deck and began rifling through the gear he found there.

There was no radio to be found. *Oh, stuff a duck,* he swore. *Where is their bloody radio?* He gave up five minutes later. Reilly was amazed that these people had spent more than seventy days in these cramped quarters. He raised his eyes toward the *Dragoon* and sighed. *Bugger!* There was nothing for it—he had to try the other vessel.

Over he went once more into the water beneath him. This time, the distance was much farther. He was completely spent, but he pushed on through nearly half a kilometre to the *Dragoon*.

This was the largest of the three vessels. Sadly, it was no better equipped. *Bollocks,* he cursed. *What do I do now?*

Woody was worried that Archie might not actually be home. What if the refugees had taken him hostage and had him locked up somewhere else? *Is the old man OK?*

The decrepit old shed sat at the bottom of the orchard on the old dirt track. You wouldn't know the cottage or shed existed if you hadn't visited it. The old track was so overgrown that poor Have-a Chat had to leave his old Ford ute on the track just below Serena's place. Any vehicle parked up there would look like it belonged to Serena or Adam.

Woody peered into the shed through the side door, which stood slightly ajar. He needed to make sure none of the refugees were there. The shed stood silent.

He wandered back over to the cottage. The old man's boots stood at the back door, a good sign that he was inside. Woody knocked lightly on the screen door and waited for a response. When there was no answer, he opened the door and cringed as it squeaked to announce this intruder. There was no reaction from within. Woody started to worry.

Stepping through the kitchen, he noted the cup of tea on the kitchen table. It was cold to his touch. Woody ventured farther into the house, moving into the lounge room. The house was quiet, with no sign of Archie.

Woody could see into the empty bedroom. He stepped inside to check the room. The bed was made. *But that could just mean the old man made his bed*, he told himself. It didn't necessarily mean he had not slept in it. *What do I do now?* he wondered.

He was startled to hear steps on the rear porch. The back door started to creak open. Woody froze. The steps came through the kitchen and into the lounge room. Any movement on the old wooden floor would give away his position. Woody had nowhere to hide. *What if it isn't Archie?* he worried.

The figure moved within sight, and the old voice boomed at him: "What the bloody hell are you doing in my bedroom?" Archie was alive and well.

"Geez, mate," laughed Woody. "I thought you were one of them."

"One of who?" snorted Archie.

"The refugees." Woody seemed puzzled that the old man didn't know what he was talking about.

"Why would I want to be one of them?" Archie quizzed him.

"You mean you don't know?" Woody scowled. "They've taken over the island. Mate, It's a nightmare."

"What are you on about, Woody?"

So Woody told him.

"Well, that explains why I couldn't find Serena. Is she all right?" Archie would just give up here and now if anything happened to his sweet girl.

"Yes, mate," Woody assured him. "She's doing great. Helping out with the kids and all up at the school."

"So what are we going to do? You say they've knocked out all communication. What about my old ham?"

"That's why I'm here, Archie," Woody explained. "We need your help."

Woody went on, "You have to contact the mainland, Archie. We don't think they know about the new boats. They certainly don't know that those bastards have taken over the island."

"Come with me." Archie smiled at Woody as he led him out the back door and down to the shed.

10

SIGNALS

"Mayday, Mayday, Mayday." Archie turned the dial to change the radio frequency and tried again, then listened for a response.

When he was investing in new equipment some years ago, Archie had insisted on a built-in general-coverage receiver inside the transceiver. That meant he could listen to short wave and also use it as a ham radio.

The transceiver was a receiver and transmitter in one unit. The controls were easier to use than the newer models with all those fancy dials. Archie didn't have the patience to sit and read a manual to figure them out. "Give me the old stuff any day" was his motto when it came to his old ham.

This short-wave variable-frequency tuning allowed Archie to move his transmitting signal in tiny increments. Hams often transmit on the same frequency. Depending on the propagation factors, they don't actually overlap one another, so they can still transmit on the same wavelength. It was slow and frustrating as he tried an array of settings.

"I keep trying, Woody," Archie told his neighbour. "I'm just not getting anything. I'm starting to think it could be the aerial. If it's not long enough, I won't get through. As I change the frequencies up, it needs a longer antenna."

He usually relied on the radar beacons up on Mount Pitt to boost his signal. Today, he would have to rely on the overhead satellites. The only problem with that was that the Internet had also been knocked out.

Without the Internet, Archie could not check on the satellite schedule for his area. He would just have to keep trying until he picked something up or they picked him up. This could take all day!

Archie turned the dial again. Still nothing! He definitely needed a longer antenna. Longer wavelengths meant lower frequencies, which meant larger antennas. There was a formula he could use to work out the length of the aerial needed. He had it written down somewhere.

"Where's that piece of paper?" He cursed his filing system.

He tore his desk apart until he found the piece of paper with his notes scrawled on it. The paper was yellow and dry with age; the ink was faded to almost illegible. The page was titled "Short wave radio propagation".

"Yes!" he cheered.

The instructions on the paper read:

> Divide 300 by the megahertz to give you the metres. Then divide that by 4 to give the length of the antenna. So, 300 divided by 148 Megahertz gives you about 2 metres; then divide that by 4 to give you 50 centimetres. That's the length of the aerial needed for 148 Megahertz.

It climbed substantially with the frequencies Archie was trying.

"Oh, stuff it," he said. "Let's just get the biggest antenna we can. That should sort it out." Woody threw the page over his shoulder onto the floor—not a great filing system at all.

He sent Woody out to find the six-metre aluminium extension ladder. Archie ran a trailing wire from the desktop ham equipment out into the yard and hooked it up to the top of the ladder. They raised the ladder to full extension and then lifted it to lean up against the cottage. Grounding the ladder on the earth would protect it from lightning strikes. The men eyed their new creation. One new antenna now in use!

"Voila! That'll do it!" Archie smirked as he strolled back to the shed.

Archie's ham pulled nearly 1,500 watts of power from his solar system. He was ready to go.

"Mayday, Mayday, Mayday!" he repeated over and over for another hour.

Crackle, crackle.

"Is that a voice?" Woody grabbed Archie's arm. "Wait, go back."

"Mayday, Mayday, Mayday."

"Launceston ham operator picking you up. What is your emergency?"

"G'day, mate." Archie smiled. "Glad to hear your voice, I can tell you!"

Have-a-chat continued. "This is Archie Jackson transmitting from Norfolk Island. We have been taken over by refugees. The locals have been corralled into the school and are being held against their will."

"Geez, what can I do to help?" said Launceston. "Yesterday's news told us you had some refugees land there, but that was all. How do a couple of hundred refugees take over an island?"

"Couple of hundred be buggered," growled Archie. "There was another thousand of the bastards turned up last night."

"OK, Archie," Launceston came back. "I'm dialling the Department of Defence phone number in Canberra as we speak. Stay with me while I talk to them, will you? By the way, my name is Rod Anderson."

"Thanks, Rod. Don't know how long we can stay open. I only have satellite connection while it's overhead. We have no phones or Internet, so I have no way of checking the satellite schedule." Archie's voice showed concern.

"OK, mate, we can fix that too," replied Rod. "Let's check that while we have you transmitting. Then I can tell you when I can call you back."

Archie could hear part of the phone conversation as Rod tried to find someone to believe him in Canberra's Defence Forces. This was going to be a hard sell. Rod was finding it hard to convince a telephone operator that an Australian island had been taken over.

"Just get me the bloody defence minister!" growled Rod at some incompetent in Canberra.

Archie could also hear Rod typing on his keyboard, so he assumed that he was on his computer searching the Internet.

"Archie?" Rod started. "We have a satellite over Norfolk again in six hours. Can you hang on until then? You seem to be beaming up from Norfolk and down to me in Tasmania, so I should be able to catch you again then."

"Yes, mate. We got nowhere to go. Talk to you then. Thanks, Rod. Over and out." Archie was shaking his head.

Crackle, crackle. The connection dropped out.

Woody looked expectantly at Archie. "What do you think?"

"I think Rod's going to have a hard time trying to convince Canberra that we need help." Archie was lost in thought. "He sounded pretty determined, though, so I guess it just takes time."

"Well," said Woody, "we've got another six hours to fill before we find out."

"Find out what?" The voice took them by surprise, frightening them into turning toward it. Reilly was standing in the doorway, staring back at them.

Reilly dried his boxers and dressed the scratches he had gotten clambering over rocks to get back onshore. He had dragged his bike back up the hill to Serena's, where it was hiding under a tarpaulin. Then he had come in search of Archie and Woody.

For the next hour, they swapped stories of the day's adventures.

"This is Wallace Marsh, secretary to Defence Minister Kellerman. How can I help you?"

Rod gave him a mouthful. There were no pleasantries attached to the conversation. It had taken Rod nearly ninety minutes talking to a variety of voices in Canberra. One of them eventually conceded to calling Secretary Marsh. It was another fifteen minutes before Marsh called Rod.

Three minutes later, Marsh hung up. He lifted his phone again and quickly dialled Lawrence Kellerman's private line. The defence minister was given the update.

Phones started squawking across Canberra as the prime minister and the chief of defence were brought up to speed. Then they hurtled orders down the line to subordinates, who were charged with implementing a recovery mission.

Canberra was on alert. Defence Radio confirmed they had picked up a small part of a transmission from Norfolk—not enough to confirm the thread of the discussion, though.

The chief of defence, Commander Annabel Bryson, had all the confirmation she needed. They had already known about the new boats arriving. They had the satellite images of the school and the guards around the perimeter. Defence Radio had been trying for hours to contact the island, to no avail. They had even tried to reposition a satellite overhead, but that took time.

Annabel already had a legion of ships on their way. It was time to hone the plan for when they arrived. Now she needed to up the ante.

HMAS *Fremantle* had been diverted from Noumea. Captain Adam Johnson had been taken by surprise at the new orders. Within hours, those orders had again changed from a refugee rescue exercise to a mission to recover the island.

He had immediately turned his vessel southward, ordering the heading changed to 29 degrees south and 167 degrees east. That would place the *Fremantle* just off Norfolk Island to await further instructions.

Captain Ewen McIntosh, onboard HMAS submarine *Kendall,* had been directing exercises off the Queensland coast. His vessel was ordered to turn eastward and divert to Norfolk.

Aircraft carrier HMAS *Townsville*, captained by Ed Havers, was ordered to cancel its involvement in the coastal exercises. The vessel turned toward Norfolk.

Navy vessel HMAS *Adelaide* had been en-route to Noumea to assist with humanitarian aid after the cyclone. Captain Jason 'Ned' Kelly was ordered to divert his massive vessel to Norfolk.

Captain Claire Oliver, onboard HMAS *Wangaratta*, ordered her vessel to depart Brisbane, bound for Norfolk.

Defence Chief Commander Annabel Bryson had updated her vessels' captains.

A large contingent of Australian navy vessels were steaming toward Norfolk Island. It would be a busy night.

"Launceston ham radio operator calling Norfolk." Rod tuned in to the same frequency. He was still some minutes ahead of the satellite returning to its position in the Pacific. He wanted to be sure to make the most of the time they were connected.

He repeated this shout-out a couple of times before the radio sprang to life. Archie's voice filled the airwaves.

"This is Norfolk ham. G'day, Rod." Archie was relieved to hear the voice from Tasmania.

"Archie, help is on its way. Those idiots at Defence say they already had an inkling that you had a problem. The first vessel will not arrive until late tonight. They expect the *Fremantle* will anchor off a place called Cascade Bay. Do you know it?"

"Sure do, mate, but how are they gonna get ashore without us to winch them onto the pier?" Archie was doubtful.

"Archie, I don't know what you mean, but they'll have rubber duckies and all kinds of stuff, so they say. They tell me they do not expect help from anybody on Norfolk. They have it under control. There's a whole bloody armada heading your way, apparently."

"Christ, I hope so. It's just a shit fight here at the moment, and we don't know where to start." Archie remained cynical.

"Archie, the *Fremantle* has been told to anchor outside the line of the horizon until the rest of the fleet arrive early tomorrow. Hang in there, mate."

"Will do." Archie looked toward Woody. "Tell me, Rod, how do I contact them when they get here?"

Rod came straight back to him. "I'm told you need to aim your torch toward Philip Island."

"Philip bloody Island?" Archie scowled "What the bloody hell for?"

"Well," said Rod, "do you know Morse Code?"

11

TORCHES

Archie, Woody, and Reilly stayed squirreled away for the remaining daylight hours. After a light supper from the dry goods in the pantry, they slept while they could.

Archie had been told in the last transmission to expect a signal around eleven in the evening. He was to be on the lookout until they made contact. It could be a long night.

It had been a while since Archie had used Morse code. He and Reilly tracked down the old Morse alphabet pamphlet in the bookcase alongside the ham. They spent hours going over the signals to refresh Archie's rusted memory. He was a little more confident but did not feel ready for what the night might bring.

Archie took some time to find his wife's old wind-up clock. Beneath her nighties in the old brown suitcase, the clock was still nestled all these years later. The suitcase had been taken to the loft a month after Irene had passed. Archie was brokenhearted every time he looked at her things. Serena had suggested moving them aside until Archie was able to deal with them. Years later, nothing had been 'dealt with'—Archie knew they never would be.

HMAS *Townsville* carried a variety of aircraft beneath deck.

At 9.00 p.m., the aircraft carrier was still some miles southwest of Norfolk. Captain Havers ordered all lights down. They could not risk being seen from Norfolk as they approached.

Personnel on deck swapped to night-vision goggles. Landing lights changed to low lights, their blue hues less visible from any great distance. Close quarters still allowed precision landing on the hard deck under low lights. Moonlight helped.

Two reconnaissance helicopters were brought to the ship's deck. The large lift doors opened for the choppers to be brought into the open air. Rotors were folded out to flying position and locked in place. Engines roared to life.

While the choppers' pilots and air navigators made the necessary calculations, the teams arrived, ready to board the aircraft. Each chopper would carry five parachutists in camouflage gear.

The choppers lifted off and headed toward Norfolk. They had to cover over sixty kilometres from the cruising aircraft carrier. The *Townsville* would continue on toward Norfolk while the choppers went in ahead of them.

Sounds carried for a greater distance at night than they did during the day. This meant the choppers needed to maintain high altitude to ensure the engine noise would not be heard from the island far below. The choppers would drop their precious cargo from a significant height to avoid detection on the island. It would be risky for the parachutists to jump from this height, but risk was part of their lives.

Their instructions were to use the unmanned airport as their drop zone. They would not have to worry about lights, as the airport was never lit up at night. Surrounding businesses would not waste electricity by illuminating their shops during the evening hours, so there would be no light from buildings nearby.

Once landed at the airport, they could spread out around the island and report back to their base. This would give them updated intel on the current situation.

Just before 10.00 p.m., the choppers were in position over the drop zone. The airfield was an easy target, even in the moonlight. One by one, they left the choppers and positioned themselves to spear toward the ground. Once clear of the choppers, rip cords were deployed and black parachutes fluttered open, slowing the descent.

Far below on Norfolk, there were no eyes honed skyward. It was naïve for the refugees to think they would not be challenged for the island, even with hostages as negotiating chips. They had not expected a rapid response from the Australian government. The refugees were not well organized. They were unprepared to defend their new territory and were busy elsewhere.

One by one, the parachutists touched down on the tarmac and scurried to release their parachutes. They abandoned their 'chutes where they landed. By morning, their existence and location would be unimportant. The men ran across to the shelter of the bodhi tree near the air terminal buildings.

Each parachutist had his compass, his radio, and his arsenal of small weapons just in case. He also had a large supply of plastic cable ties to use as wrist restraints.

Personnel disappeared across the paddocks in different directions. The map of Norfolk had been carved up into quadrants. They would search out the refugees and gather information on how they were organised.

Their mission was reconnaissance, but they expected to come face to face with some refugees. Once subdued, refugees would be restrained using the cable ties on wrists and ankles. Watch out, any refugee who got in their way!

One team was sent to the school. They would report back on the number of guards on the perimeter. The school team would then work their way out to the guide hall, to establish it as their base.

Another team was sent to the township. They were to advise on refugee movements in town and around the town hall. They were responsible for assessing the threat from the refugees' leadership team.

Two teams were sent to secure the piers at Cascade Bay to the north and Kingston to the south of the island.

The final two-man team was sent to Headstone Tip—the only other site on the island where there was a pier of sorts. It was a concrete deck used to incinerate the island's refuse. Tonight it would have a different use.

Along the way, each team was to check out any farmhouse for refugees. Any who were captured were to be taken to Salty Theatre. The site of the weekly theatre performance of *Mutiny on the Bounty* was outside in the open. It already had a perimeter fence, seating, and basic facilities.

Information—on refugee numbers, vehicles, and weapons—was to be relayed back to the team at the guide hall as the morning progressed.

This intel would become the basis for the plan being formulated to take back the island.

At 10.00 p.m., *Townsville* anchored behind Philip Island. A landing party was quickly despatched in a rubber duckie. They manoeuvred along the eastern shore of Philip Island to find a landing site. Among some rocky crags, a little pebble beach came into sight. Three sailors stepped ashore. One started the ascent

toward the high peak of the island. He had his signal box with him.

As he clambered over the rocks, he was thankful he had learnt that the locals had cleared this outpost landmass of feral animals. Previous military personnel had used Philip Island as a hunting ground. They had introduced wild pigs, goats, and rabbits as sporting targets. Feral animals had ravaged the island for over a hundred years before the locals implemented a cull. Then they began a reforestation programme.

These small bushes now gave cover to the signalman.

Even Reilly was exhausted. The swim had sapped him of his energy. The alarm woke the trio at 10.45 p.m.

Archie's old eyes were not what they once had been, and he nearly missed the flashing signal in the moonlight.

"Archie, look!" Reilly cried out excitedly as the first flash of light came to them from the apex of Philip Island.

"D-E-D," Archie spoke aloud as he read the letters being signalled to him.

Woody's brow furled in question. "Huh? DED—Christ, I hope not."

Archie went straight back to the signalman with "N-E-E-D R-E-P-E-A-T".

Back it came in flashes through the night: "S-C-O-U-T P-A-R-T-Y L-A-N-D-E-D".

A cheer went up among the three men, who whooped the air and slapped one another on the back. "Yee-haa!" cried Archie.

"Wait," said Reilly. "There's more."

"S-H-I-P-S D-U-E B-E-F-O-R-E D-A-W-N W-I-L-L R-E-C-L-A-I-M I-S-L-A-N-D W-A-R-N L-O-C-A-L-S".

"W-I-L-L D-O" Archie winked back to them.

"Done," called Reilly as he headed out the door. "Looks like I'm going back to school." Now he had to sneak back in!

"Good luck," called Woody as he saw him off.

12

COUNTDOWN

Reilly had plenty of cover in the midnight hours. Strolling up the track from Archie's, he made his way back to Serena's. He pulled the tarpaulin back, dragged the bike out from underneath it, and jumped aboard. The bike seat was hard, but he had only a short way to pedal. Ten minutes was all it would take.

A couple of kilometres along Rooty Hill Road, Reilly spun the wheels around the left-hand corner onto Collins Head Road. He would pull the bike into Cutters Corn Lane behind the school and make his way from there. There was no other traffic in the area. House lights had been extinguished for the night. Even the cows were asleep in the paddocks. A lone rooster crowed in the distance.

Reilly had wagged school many times and had no trouble escaping the classroom. He had never before had to break back in! He was a little stumped. Most would be asleep by now, so few would be visiting the bathrooms. How could he let them know he needed cover to get back inside with them?

He didn't have long to think about it. He was at the pine grove behind the school, stowing his bike in the shadow of the tall trees before he knew it. As he turned toward the school, he walked straight into the web of "community spiders".

Golden orbs are large nonvenomous spiders, and they have long inhabited Norfolk Island. They weave monstrously big webs that are left undisturbed for years. Called community spiders because every community has them, they're left alone by the locals.

Reilly spluttered an expletive as he swiped the cobwebs from his face and chest. He could feel a hefty spider climbing up his arm. He shivered, the hairs on his arms standing tall in response. Reilly brushed the spiders away until he was free of the web and then strode on through the pine trees.

At the school-yard fence, he could see the shrubs nearby. He stopped to watch and listen for refugee guards in the area. All was quiet. In fact, he could hear snoring nearby.

As he inched his way across the yard, the snoring got louder. Reilly could see a body shape asleep on the grass near the water tanks. He stopped and waited until he knew the refugee guard was not going to waken.

Reilly smiled to himself as he inched past the sleeping guard. He worked his way back around the water tanks to the door of the boy's toilets. Approaching footsteps stopped him in his tracks. *Shit! What to do?* He started to tremble.

The footsteps were close now, and Reilly knew they were about to round the corner right in front of him. He turned into the door of the toilet block.

"Hey you," the guard yelled. "What are you doing?"

Reilly's head was over the toilet bowl. He was throwing up.

The guard came up behind him. The single overhead light bulb showed Reilly's frame bent low over the bowl. Heaving sounds told the story.

Reilly was praying over the bowl, "Oh god, oh god." He slowly rose and turned to face the guard. Wiping the spew from his mouth, it was obvious that Reilly was genuinely unwell.

The guard grabbed him roughly by the arm and propelled him back toward the staff room opposite. "Get back inside."

Reilly had not known that fear would make him throw up.

Back inside, Reilly was roughly propelled into the staff room. He took a blanket from the side table as he entered and spread it on the floor as bedding.

Outside, Reilly could hear the guard rousing his sleeping companion. There was a diatribe of abuse directed at the other refugee guard, who had been asleep. Reilly smiled like a contented cat!

As he settled on the hard wood floor, Reilly looked across at his sleeping buddies.

Alongside him, Vince stirred and rolled over. He stretched and briefly opened his eyes. Consciousness came quickly when he realised he was looking at Reilly, who was smiling back at him.

"What the hell are you doing here?" Vince whispered.

"Got a message for you." Reilly smirked. "The troops are here!"

The smile spread across Vince's face. "No shit?"

"No shit!" replied Reilly, smiling smugly.

Within minutes, the room was awake and whispering. They were huddled around Reilly, listening intently to his tales of the day's adventures.

"Oh, that's fantastic. Well done." Maggie was very excited. "What about Archie and Woody?"

"They've got a few chores to take care of, but they're on cloud nine." Reilly was pleased to be able to deliver this information.

Archie and Woody had succeeded, and the navy was there. Reilly had little other information for them. He did not know the details, just that they should be prepared for some excitement during the day.

The others had lots of questions. How did they manage it? Who was there? How were they going to free them?

"I'm sorry, but I don't have those answers. We just have to sit tight until they get to us. They have to secure the island first, and that means finding all the refugees. I have no idea how long that will take." Reilly was becoming quite the leader.

They had to get a message to the other locals locked away in classrooms across the school grounds. There would be lots of trips to the bathroom in the next few hours.

Nobody went back to sleep, even though sunrise was still hours away.

The invasion of the school was scheduled for dawn.

13

Just before sundown, HMAS *Fremantle* downed anchors north of Norfolk Island. According to the naval charts, they had anchored fifty kilometres northwest of Cascade Bay. They were out of sight of the island.

It would take the *Fremantle* about two hours to move to their target site. From there, they would launch a landing party. They needed cover of darkness, but they also needed reinforcements. More vessels were on their way. The wait began.

At Cascade Bay, the *Fremantle* sailed into sight just before midnight. They dropped anchor just a kilometre offshore; they were nestled in between the refugee boats. A landing party was quickly dispatched to the pier.

Five enormous rubber duckies arrived in the first wave. The men scrambled onto the pier in droves and clambered up the hill. The first homes reclaimed were those sitting above the pier overlooking Cascade Bay. Two hundred and fifty sailors were heading across the northeastern area of the island.

Special Force sailors moved eastward to round up refugees. In the area from Simon's Water down along Stockyard Road, they raided homes one by one. They searched farms and rummaged outbuildings to ensure they located all refugees. They marshalled the refugees into parkland at the end of Two Chimneys Road overlooking the cliffs.

The second wave of rubber duckies arrived at Cascade pier. This group was responsible for scouring homes and farms on the way into Burnt Pine Township. They scoured Harpers Road, rounding up refugees as they went. The area behind the Bottle House in the valley near the school was used to isolate this group of refugees.

A second group of 250 sailors headed toward town. All were used to working silently, so tonight would not challenge them. Hand signals worked well.

⟋

By 2.00 a.m., HMAS *Adelaide* had anchored off Puppy's Point on Norfolk's west coast.

Their first landing party was sent to Anson beach. This beach was renowned for rough water, and the sailors suffered heavy seas trying to land. Over a hundred seamen were forced to clamber up the donkey trail that formed the only track to the top of the cliff.

From there, the servicemen and women dispersed across the western coast. They were responsible for the area from Anson Bay north to Duncombe Bay and across to Captain Cook Road. They would commandeer farm vehicles, cars, and trucks for transport. They fanned out across the northwest corner of the island.

Once located, the refugees from this area were to be taken back to the Captain Cook Monument parkland. There, they would be isolated until the island had been reclaimed.

The *Adelaide* sent another landing party across to Headstone Tip. They would use the small concrete dock to get onto the island.

Two hundred sailors clambered up onto Norfolk Island at Headstone. They split into groups and veered off across the island. Some groups went left onto Headstone Road. They would comb the area up to the Maze and then push inland toward town.

Another group would push right onto New Farm Road. From here they would work their way around the southern perimeter of the airport. They were responsible for the area from Headstone right across to Country Road.

Part of the group peeled off and headed up Ferny Lane, back toward town.

HMAS *Kendall* arrived off Cemetery Bay on Norfolk's east coast at 4.00 a.m. The submarine surfaced, and a dozen divers appeared on the rounded deck. Each slipped overboard into the dark waters and headed ashore to land on the small beach beneath the golf course.

These divers were sent as a scouting party. They discarded diving gear and wetsuits on the sand at Cemetery Bay. The divers used the cover of the pine trees lining the fairways as they made their way up the greens of the golf course. They could not be seen from the high ground above the bay.

As they manoeuvred across the fairways up onto Quality Row, their progress looked stage managed. Effortlessly, they moved across to Middlegate Road and headed up past the new barracks of the World Heritage area.

Following this road up the hill, they were searching for the guide hall. This was the base they needed near the school, to coordinate the raid.

In the subtropical environs, dawn will not arrive until just after 6.45 a.m. The hours before dawn were full of chaos for the refugees.

Along the northwest quadrant, 161 refugees had been intercepted. They were dragged from beds by sailors dressed in camouflage. The refugees were confronted by faces covered in night-vision goggles. There was a futuristic feel to the sailors' attire, and it was frightening in its simplicity.

Women screamed, babies cried, toddlers cowered behind parent's legs in the half-light of morning.

Rifles were raised, cable ties produced. Adult mouths were taped with gaffer tape.

There was no conversation, just force without violence.

A procession of refugees began the trek up Captain Cook Road. Their numbers swelled as the navy teams searched out more homes, more farms, and more refugees.

The refugees were outnumbered, isolated, and secured.

By 4.15 a.m. this quadrant had been reclaimed.

Salty Theatre was quickly filling with refugees subdued from within the lower western quadrant.

Norfolk Blue Stud Farm relinquished over a dozen refugees. One teenager made it out of the window of the farmhouse below the restaurant. He had heard muffled noises coming from the bedroom next door. Floorboards had squeaked along the hallway. It was out of place at 4.30 a.m. The kid bolted out the window.

He tumbled onto the grass driveway and scrambled to his feet. He raced up the fence line and slipped across the road into the Hundred Acres woodland. Sixty seconds later, he would have come face to face with sailors coming up New Farm Road from Headstone Tip.

As it was, they saw him dash across the roadway. He disappeared into the woods.

Three sailors took off after him, running in hot pursuit. They had the advantage of night-vision goggles and experience in the dark. He had the advantage of a full minute's head start.

The forest was thick woodland infested with community spiders. The kid ran headlong into an expanse of previously undisturbed cobwebs. It was a mass of silk-like ribbons strung three metres high between the trees.

He yelled and started swiping at the cobwebs, disturbing the golden orb spiders in their home. The angry arachnids headed toward the source of the vibration. They needed to defend their space.

The sailors had lost sight of him before they got into the woodlands. Training told them to stop and wait to hear the kid's footsteps. The sailors got their sense of direction from the kid's screams and headed toward him in the dark.

The kid heard them coming up on him. He turned but could not see them; he had not realised they were dressed in camouflage gear. His feet had become tangled in a vine that trailed across the forest floor. He tripped. Another grunting yelp escaped him and echoed into the night. The kid fell hard against a tree before bouncing onto the ground.

A hand reached out and yanked him back to his feet. He was barely a metre and a half tall. This lanky kid with acned skin was no threat. They harnessed his hands anyway and taped his mouth to shut him up. The kid had started to scream again.

Back on New Farm Road, the procession of refugees had started to form. They were being herded to the outdoor theatre. There were 218 pairs of feet tramping the road. They were surrounded by navy teams.

Along Ferny Lane, toward Burnt Pine Township, the navy teams were scouring homes and farms. They had rounded up forty-seven refugees before they got to the main road. These refugees had been walked back across the airport tarmacs, then down toward the church and on to the outdoor theatre. It was the shortest path to get them out of town quickly.

The next target was the hospital. With a handful of wards and consulting rooms, the hospital offered good accommodation for seventeen families. One by one, the rooms were searched and secured. Special Forces teams were careful not to cause any damage to the equipment in the wards. Oxygen tanks were protected lest they get damaged—they could explode. Refugees streamed out of the hospital and onto the roadway. They followed in the footsteps of the last group, back across the airport.

This brought the total count so far to a few short of five hundred refugees. The navy teams were making good progress. It was now 4.45 a.m.

Just before the rays of the sun started peeking above the horizon, Archie was awake. He and Woody had set the old wind-up alarm clock for 4.45 a.m. It shrilled at them right on time. Both men fell to their feet, startled by the bell.

They did not know if they would be contacted again. They did not know who, what, or where; they did know when, and dawn was fast approaching.

As the first light spread across the eastern sky, the men could just make out movement on the water across Slaughter Bay.

They walked up the track to Serena's, where Woody helped Archie push Serena's little car out of the driveway. Archie jumped into the driver's seat to steer then let the car roll down the hill and around the corner near the lookout. It continued on silently, down toward Kingston Pier. The car petered out of momentum just before the end of the Commons. Archie left the vehicle there and waited for Woody.

Woody snuck back across the road to his place, mindful of any noise that might disturb the refugees sleeping in his bed. He easily opened the back shed. He was thankful that he had fixed the squeaking hinges last summer, so his movements were essentially silent.

The four-wheel drive was facing the driveway, on a downward incline. Woody hopped behind the driver's wheel and released the hand brake. The vehicle started to inch forward and gradually gained momentum as it slid out of the driveway. Woody let it roll down the hill to where Archie stood waiting.

Woody left the keys in the ignition after parking the vehicle alongside the pier store and walked back to Archie.

They drove Serena's little car back up the hill to within sight of Woody's place.

This time, Woody snuck his wife's station wagon out of the driveway and down to the Kingston Pier. Archie rolled Serena's car down the hill behind Woody, then drove them both back up the hill to collect another vehicle.

Woody inched the back gates open behind his shed. Archie helped him to push the flat-top truck out onto the road. It too made it down to Kingston Pier within minutes.

Back up the hill, they went back to Serena's for her fiancé Adam's four-wheel drive. Down it went to Kingston Pier. Then the mini bus Archie had brought home for yesterday's tours also went down to Kingston, followed by Serena's little car.

They left the vehicles there, along with a map of the island on the front seat of each vehicle, compliments of Norfolk Island Tourist Bureau. They walked back up the hill. It was hard going for a couple of sleep-deprived seniors. It was a small but steep hill, yet they were back at Archie's half an hour later.

The two men were pleased with their efforts. It might speed up the process once the landing party made it onto the pier.

The torch came out, and Archie began to signal across to Philip Island. A lone signalman read the message and relayed it to the *Townsville*.

"L-E-F-T K-E-Y-S I-N S-I-X C-A-R-S A-T K-I-N-G-S-T-O-N".

By 5.00 a.m., HMAS *Wangaratta* could be seen in the distant half-light of morning, far beyond Nepean Island. It was steaming in to anchor near Point Hunter.

The rubber duckies from the *Wangaratta* would scoot across to Lone Pine, just off Emily Bay. The heavy-duty material used to construct these vessels ensured they would withstand a multitude of conditions—rocks would not challenge them. Sailors were unloaded, and the duckies returned to the *Wangaratta* for more and more personnel.

Within an hour, five hundred sailors from the *Wangaratta* had been landed on Norfolk. They were to secure the southeast corner of the island. This area was bounded by Kingston town, up Taylors Road and across to Collins Head Road. Any refugees found in this region would be pushed across to Garnet Point for isolation.

From the other end of the island, the navy teams from the *Fremantle* were increasing the total head count. They made steady progress across the island, rounding up refugees as they went.

The sailors moved stealthily across the northern quadrant from Simons Water. A small team surrounded and watched each farmhouse for a full two minutes. They wanted to avoid any unexpected reactions from pets. Dogs yelping in the night would wake the sleeping refugees.

When a team was confident that they knew the basic layout of a building, they moved in. There was little activity in any farmhouse at this hour until the seamen tackled each target.

No house was ever locked on Norfolk - it was a throwback to the 1950s, when neighbours were trusted. Sailors simply opened a door and walked up a hallway to find sleeping refugees. The largest were cornered first, then the smaller ones. One by one, families were rounded up. They were handcuffed with cable ties and their mouths gaffer taped. No sense risking an alert to the next farm by screams that would carry in the night.

They added another three hundred and ninety seven to their count by isolating them at picnic grounds at Two Chimneys Road. A hundred and fifty sailors stayed to guard them. If the refugees wanted to escape, the only way out was over the cliffs. They were welcome to try.

When the northern quadrant was cleared of refugees, the teams of sailors split up. One group headed down Cascade Road. Now devoid of human trespassers, the area belonged to the navy teams.

One hundred sailors stayed at the soft drink factory, a few hundred metres from the school. They waited for the signal to proceed. The area to the south of the school had not yet been secured. Dawn was slowly approaching.

The other fifty sailors made their way across toward Harper Road, heading into town. They joined the second landing party from the *Fremantle*.

The job was about to get a whole lot trickier. As they moved closer to town, they started to come across the island's tourist accommodations. This meant there were a lot more beds to be cleared, a lot more refugees to be isolated and contained.

Sailors could exclude tourists from their concerns. The tourists had already been taken to the school along with the locals. Woody had confirmed this.

Holiday apartments in Norfolk were often built back from the road. Long driveways led into wide car-parks that housed hire cars. That gave little cover for the sailors coming up the gravel driveway. Thankfully, the grass was soft along the edge of the driveway. It hid the noise of their footsteps.

Windows had been left open to cool the apartments. It was the only way to release the heat that had been trapped inside all day. Sailors slid doors open or stepped through open windows to gain entry. They found the bedrooms and stood over sleeping forms.

When eyes first stirred open, the shock of a human form standing over them was enough to instil fear. Across each apartment, refugees sat bolt upright in the dark. Their mouths were covered with tape before they could scream or cuss. Hands were dragged behind them and then cuffed. They were dragged out of bed and propelled into the night before they had time to realise what was happening. Children were carried in the arms of the sailors.

As the teams moved closer to town, they inspected offices and businesses as well. Empty buildings awaited them at the police station, radio station, and the library.

Sailors covered the restaurants on the western side. Teams moved slowly into the township until they made it to the centre of town. The northern team turned the corner of the main street at the island's only roundabout.

From here, they would head southeast to search the holiday apartments in this remaining area of town. This included the zone along Queen Elizabeth Drive toward the school. There were a lot of apartments and motels in this area. It was one of the most heavily populated tourist areas on the island. Inhabitants of this zone would be pushed back out of town to the Bottle House marshalling area. This area had to be cleared without those at the school detecting the activity.

One small group of sailors moved behind the bowling club to clear the Aloha Apartments.

In the distance, they could see supporting teams moving toward them from the hospital end of town.

The hospital team was headed to the community hall but did not expect any inhabitants at this hour. A wristwatch showed 5.15 a.m.

At 5.25 a.m., the first teams from the *Wangaratta* were ticking off houses in the southeastern quadrant of Norfolk. The terrain was hilly, and the farmhouses were more spread out along this part of the island.

The refugees were outnumbered by three to one. The sailors barely missed a heartbeat in rounding up the foreigners from this part of the community.

Garnet Point was quickly filling. It was 6.05 a.m.

Archie and Woody paced up and down. From their vantage point, they could see movement down at Kingston pier. They could not tell the size of the contingent that had been landed so far. They were watching shadows.

The half dozen vehicles they had taken down to the pier store vanished one by one. None came up the hill past Serena's place. They saw her little car heading up past the lights of the government buildings at Kingston, up Middlegate Road toward the guide hall. The headlights had been switched off.

Archie hated the waiting. He knew it was only a matter of time before the refugees in Woody's house were captured. Some nearby farms had also been inhabited by foreigners. It would take time to clear them as well. Until then, any light from the guide hall could be seen across the valley. That was if anyone was awake at this time of the morning.

Woody stayed in the shed with Archie. They did not want to leave the little ham radio, in case they were needed. From the shed, they had a good view across to Philip Island if another signal was flashed at them. Waiting was torture.

Archie got up from his chair and walked back to the window. Woody, leaning against the window frame, was staring out to sea.

As the men stared together, a face popped up in the window. The men jumped back, their natural response to the unexpected. The face at the window lifted his mask and smiled at them. The navy had found them.

Behind them, the shed door creaked open, and another face smiled in their direction.

The group huddled together for fifteen minutes as Woody and Archie told the sailors all they knew about the layout of the school. The sailors drew a mud map—a simple representation of the buildings and the classrooms at the school. Woody added information about the guards and confirmed that the tourists were also being held at the school.

Questions were asked about the leader of the refugees. How could they identify him? Woody was able to give them a detailed description.

Then they all left together to go to the base camp—the day was about to begin.

The sky began to lighten more quickly now. Archie glanced at his old clock—it showed 6.10 a.m.

At Kingston pier, the teams from HMAS *Townsville* were brought ashore. The aircraft carrier had amphibious warfare landing craft to enable it to land a thousand personnel.

The advance party took advantage of the vehicles sitting parked near the pier store. They would thank Archie later.

Their numbers were split into task forces. Three hundred were sent into town to reclaim the township. There, they would meet up with the other naval forces already in situ and waiting for them.

It was now just before 6.15 a.m. Dawn was still over half an hour away.

Twenty three hundred and twenty two sailors were moving like ants across the island

Back in town, a burning cigarette signalled refugees were in attendance at the hall.

There was a group of about twenty. The conversation was around plans for the coming days and weeks. They wanted to tell their families and friends to join them. They had not yet had the opportunity to do so. Instead, they had been consumed with sorting out the locals and assuming the running of the island.

They had not even buried the child who had perished in the water off Emily Bay. They must do that today.

In the early morning hours, they brought their prayer mats as they gathered for dawn prayers.

Abbud wanted some alone time to take in the events of the last days—he walked outside to smoke, well away from the others.

The supermarkets had surrendered their tobacco hauls earlier in the day.

Abbud was thankful for the quiet of the early morning. It had been a busy couple of days. The locals had given them more trouble than he had expected. His thoughts reflected the events of the previous day.

He had originally sent 150 guards to the school but later revised that to more than 380. They were there around the clock.

Over the first twenty-four hours, the locals had eventually settled down. They had finally realised the refugees owned the island. While they weren't happy about it, the locals could do no more than accede. Nobody wanted to risk life or limb.

The cigarette was again raised to Abbud's lips. The embers glowed brighter as Abbud inhaled. He drew deeply on the cigarette and enjoyed the lingering smoke before exhaling.

As he lowered his arm to his side, the glow of the cigarette receded. It was not strong enough to illuminate the hand that came in over the top of his own. The half-smoked cigarette fell to the ground.

Abbud spun around as another hand wrapped around his torso. He was quickly subdued by two men in camouflage gear. Their hideous goggles made them look like black pigs in the moonlight. Abbud fought back until he was hit over the head with the butt of a rifle.

His body slumped, and his head ached as he fell to the ground. He was conscious—just!

The men spun his hands behind his back and cuffed them with cable ties. Abbud was incapable of fighting back in this state of half-awareness. His feet were next. They were immobilised with cable ties. His voice was lost behind a strip of gaffer tape.

There was a scuffle inside the hall. Fifty sailors had advanced together. Fists flew as refugees tried to defend themselves. It was a futile exercise. Surprised by the sudden and unexpected onslaught, they were lost. The refugees were outnumbered. Feet slipped on prayer mats, and bodies hit the floor. One old man tried to escape through a side door. He was soon caught and restrained.

The total count was steadily growing. The numbers were radioed back to the guide hall at 6.15 a.m.

Down at Kingston Pier, a thousand servicemen and women had gathered on the Common. *Townsville*'s large group were split into five working parties. They brought ashore a supply of barbed-wire fencing to secure the isolation camps around the island.

A series of mini buses driven by navy personnel started to arrive at the Heritage site. They would be used to drive around the perimeter roads away from the school. There was no concern now that the vehicles might alert the refugees. Two-way radios had confirmed the refugees had been isolated and secured—all except for the guards at the school.

When the isolation camps were cordoned off, the working parties would separate. Half of each group would help guard the camps and set up supply tents and toilet blocks. The other half would head back to the school.

The only remaining invaders were at the school in the centre of the island. But not for long!

Early scouting parties had indicated that the number of refugee guards surrounding the school had been reduced. First satellite photos had shown an estimated 350 guards surrounding the school. Today, the scouts estimated this had dropped to just 120.

The guards kept moving, which made it hard for the locals to get an accurate count. Most had beards, so they all looked alike.

None of the locals wanted to upset the status quo until they had a solid plan. The navy beat them to it.

In the predawn, they whispered to one another about the impending defence retaliation. The staff room was a hive of gossip, but they had no way of letting the others know. They hadn't crossed paths with anyone in the loos in the previous few hours.

"It could be for the best," Maggie declared. "We don't want anyone to give the game away."

She looked at her watch. It was 6.25 a.m.

14

DAWN

Light from the rising sun started to fill the guide hall. The day was going to be warm and steamy. Storm clouds still swirled overhead—the threat of rain was obvious.

The final numbers were in from the scouting parties. These were compared to the numbers counted by the locals. Woody knew the final count of refugees because he had been operating the crane at Cascade Bay. He had counted every one of them ashore and then added that number to the morning's count.

So the Navy SEALs now knew that somewhere on the island were seventeen refugees who were unaccounted for. That was assuming the numbers guarding the school were correct.

If refugees had been missed, it would be in the area beneath Mount Pitt. A scouting party was sent back to find them.

In the guide hall, the team leaders were being briefed. Lights burned brightly now. They could not be seen from the school. Two-way radios were squawking around the island as orders were issued from the guide hall.

From the north, the team waiting at the soft-drink factory started their forward charge. They would proceed to the edge of the school yard along the pine grove on the eastern border.

The group holding refugees at the Bottle House would split. Some would remain to guard the refugees until the barbed-wire fences were installed. The others would convene at the Uniting Church, across the road from the school. They could cross the fields to get there without being seen from the school.

From the south, the team from the *Wangaratta* would move up to the PlayCentre on the corner of the crossroads.

The teams that landed at Anson Bay and Headstone Tip offered up groups to join the charge on the school. They would meet at the Catholic Church. From there, they would climb over the fence into the Uniting Church.

Everybody was in place. The time was 6.40 a.m.

"Go, go, go" was bawled down the radios.

The sailors came silently out of their hiding positions and swarmed onto the school grounds.

At the back of the school, the pine grove came alive. Camouflaged sailors looked like tree trunks until they moved. They swarmed over the little wooden fence.

They had been watching for a while now—waiting for the signal to come—so they had time to count the guards on this side of the school. Each sailor was to focus on a particular guard. They were to bring them down silently. No noise was to be heard from the front of the building. No risks were to be taken while the other sailors moved into place. The safety of the hostages was their paramount concern.

On this side of the school grounds, there were fifteen guards. They were awake and ready for morning prayers. Colourful prayer mats were spread on the ground; refugees bent to kneel on them as the sun glinted above the horizon. A twig snapped nearby, and the guards looked up toward the pine grove. *Shit!*

They were crash tackled so fast, there was no time for them to respond. Mouths were covered and limbs tied. Navy SEALs kept the refugee guards on the ground. Each guard had three sailors on him—one on either side and one behind. They were frog-marched back to the pine grove.

From the Uniting Church, one small group of Navy SEALs would charge the front gate of the school. The driveway led to the teachers' carpark and into the Administration Block. They were to take the staff-room guards - they had counted only three guards around this building, but there could be more.

The other SEAL teams would move to the south of the school buildings. This would allow them to storm the classrooms. Their approach would be hidden until the last second on this side.

There were fourteen classrooms in all. Each was guarded by a team of seven—a total of ninety-eight guards on this side of the school. All had to be taken simultaneously. Prayer time would leave them most exposed and unprepared to defend themselves.

Fremantle's team was in place now along the northern perimeter. They had a watch-and-see alert. Their responsibility was to ensure no refugee guard escaped. As was often the case, there was usually someone in the bathroom or asleep out of sight. They would scour the grounds starting at the perimeter fence. When they had secured the grounds, they could help with the guards in the classrooms.

It was the most excitement the sailors had experienced in years. Real live action.

Inside the staff room, Vince waited for the sound of approaching footsteps. He could not know whether they were friend or foe. When the footsteps came, it was Hassan who stood in the doorway. Vince stared at him.

Hassan wanted to check on them before he went to prayers. He surveyed the room, nodded to his young compatriot who would stay to watch the hostages, then turned away and locked the door behind him. As he turned back toward the carpark, he was subdued from behind. A yelp escaped his lips before his mouth could be covered.

Two sailors had been in the hallway watching him from the broom closet. Woody's info had been correct. They had snuck in, one at a time, through the trap-door in the floor. They had to catch Hassan before he fell to the floor. They did not want a sound to disturb the guards on the other side of the door. They could not risk the hostages being harmed by refugee guards alerted to an attack.

Outside, the other guards were waiting for Hassan. When the door opened, they expected to see him. Instead, they saw masked faces. Their attention was consumed by the unexpected sight. They were totally unaware of the four men looming behind them. There was little struggle before they were subdued.

With limbs strapped and mouths taped, these guards were now under control. They were taken back across the road to the Uniting Church. Navy teams were guarding the church, where the refugees would be kept under lock and key.

Inside the staff room Maggie had chosen the darkest corner of the room for her grand-daughter to get some sleep. She had been glad of Serena's company - and happy to know there was another set of eyes on the little one when Maggie needed a bathroom break.

The women had watched as the younger guard, ogling Serena throughout the day, had inched closer to her as the evening progressed. The guy was creepy – almost stalking Serena.

When the scuffle broke out at the door of the staff room, the guard was suddenly alert to the commotion, his eyes off Serena for the first time in hours. He raised his rifle and aimed it toward the door. Vince stepped in front of him, but was roughly pushed aside. Serena, standing behind the guard, picked up a chair and hit him over the head with it. He dropped to the floor – he was out cold.

Maggie stared wide-eyed at Serena, who put the chair down and said "Oh, that felt good!"

The two women burst out laughing. The locals were quickly alongside them, tying the limbs of the refugee guard, to stop any further movement. His rifle was quickly garnered and aimed at him, not that he would know that until he came back to consciousness.

The scene outside the classrooms was orderly. There were nearly twenty Navy SEALs for each classroom. They were paired off and assigned to target specific guards.

As the rays of sun reflected across the sky, the light signalled the final assault. The silent count was seen on the hands of the team leader. *Three. Two. One. NOW!*

Feet scarpered around the classrooms. The guards inside were preparing for morning devotions. As they started to shake out their little prayer mats to spread on the floor, the classroom doors disintegrated. The final push of sailors erupted into classrooms across the school grounds.

Scuffles broke out as sailors subdued refugees. Locals and tourists were quickly awake and screaming. Terror was caused by surprise. It soon quietened when they realised they were being rescued.

Refugees were shuffled into corners, cuffed then marched outside. There was no quiet now. No need for gags; the surprise was complete.

The scene was being repeated in rooms across the grounds, and the last of the refugees were quickly taken.

Applause broke out in classrooms. Locals cheered, and tourists cried with relief.

On the northern perimeter of the school yard, a sleeping guard was roused by the noise. As he opened his eyes and looked up, a rifle butt appeared in his face. He blinked. The face above him sneered smugly. Cable ties were produced, gaffer tape employed, and the prisoner lifted to his feet.

Behind him, a refugee came out of the bathroom. He was greeted with two rifles aimed at his head. He thought he might need the bathroom again. Fear will do that!

From the pine grove, refugees were marched across the playground and through the carpark. Across the road, they were led into the Uniting Church.

A handful of refugees were delivered from the staff room and from the grounds. The rest were rounded up from the classrooms. They were herded across the road—the church was filling fast. At least they had pews to sit on!

Relieved locals and tourists flooded into the school's playground. They were still stunned, but all were OK.

Outside, a corps of nearly five hundred sailors were exuberant. A radio crackled into life. "Island secured, sir."

The chorus went up around him as cheers broke the dawn at 6.47 a.m.

15

ULTIMATUM

In the following daylight hours, the level of activity increased. Across the island, prisoners were confined to wire enclosures—they were well guarded.

The fleet, positioned around the island, was waiting for instructions from the mainland. *How to proceed?*

Locals spent over an hour talking through their harrowing ordeal. They swapped stories and commiserated with one another. They tried to persuade the tourists to come back for a real holiday. Their efforts would prove to be in vain.

This beautiful little island paradise would never be quite the same again. Locals felt betrayed for opening their doors. They had just wanted to be hospitable to the newcomers.

❧

Up on Mount Pitt, the navy crews went to work. There were six towers to be restored before communications could be reconnected.

Radio and telephone specialists started working at the telecommunications base at Anson Bay. Their first priority was to reconnect the phones and Internet. Without these, the island could not resume business activities. Hundreds of locals wanted to call family and friends on the mainland. It would be days before that happened.

At the airport, the naval engineers were inspecting the runways. The tarmac had been torn up only partway through its solid base. The top layer had been decimated, but the reinforced concrete base was still intact. It was not as bad as they had thought it might be. They brought in the road maintenance team to work on repairing it. This would prove difficult until they could get their hands on loads of tar and gravel. They were unsure if there was enough on the island to repair the damage.

The communication beacons around the airport were also inspected. A list of replacement parts was drawn up. Captain Ed Havers, aboard the *Townsville*, sent the list through to the mainland. It would be several days before they could be delivered. Once the parts arrived from Europe, they would be flown to the island. The small plane would land on the flight deck of *Townsville.*

Problems have a way of resolving themselves once the right resources are thrown at them. The only remaining problem they had now was the refugees. *What to do with them?*

Prime Minister William Stephenson sent his congratulations to all teams involved. He was full of praise for Defence Chief Annabel Bryson for her foresight. Had she not sent her forces to Norfolk when she did, the outcome could have been vastly different. Another twenty-four hours, and the locals and tourists would have been forced onto refugee boats. They would have been condemned to an almost hopeless fate at sea.

Defence Minister Laurence Kellerman recommended Annabel for an Order of Australia Medal.

Commendations were awarded to the captains of the vessels sent to Norfolk. Their quick response to this crisis was greatly appreciated. They had shown great leadership in organising their teams—the operational side of the landing had been exemplary. The reclamation of Norfolk would be seen as legendary in years to come.

In turn, the captains heaped praise on their teams. Each had performed extremely well. Difficult tasks had been handled with aplomb. In particular, the silent attacks had given them the upper hand in reclaiming the island. They could all be proud.

When the excitement of the morning settled down, there was still one question unanswered. *What do we do with the refugees?*

Prime Minister Stephenson called the chief justice of the Supreme Court of Australia. Their discussion, on a point of law, lasted for over an hour. Recommendations were made and accepted. They would have to be relayed to the chief minister on Norfolk.

Captain Ed Havers was asked to bring Norfolk's chief minister out to the *Townsville* to speak directly with the prime minister.

"Permission to come aboard?" Chief Minister Harrison Paul requested as he stepped aboard the *Townsville.*

"Permission granted" was the response from Captain Havers. "Welcome, sir. I trust you are well?"

"Perfectly well, thanks to the Australian navy." Harrison was more than delighted to meet Captain Havers in person. The hand shaking lasted some time. There was real gratitude behind the gesture.

"This way if you would, please, sir." Havers directed.

The chief minister followed him along the deck and in through an open door. He was escorted to the captain's boardroom. Morning tea had been set out on the boardroom table.

"Please make yourself at home, Chief Minister. We will place the call to the prime minister once you are settled in." Havers was the perfect host.

"Thank you, Prime Minister. Yes, I fully understand. I will deliver the edict myself." Harrison wasn't surprised at the decision. He understood it and agreed with it.

The law is the law, Harrison reflected as he was escorted back across the bay to Norfolk Island. He would relay the decision to Norfolk's legislative assembly first. The Council of Nine were waiting on the outcome of this morning's discussion.

The councillors had convened at the public library—few could stomach the thought of going back to the town hall. They greeted the chief minister and took their places around a hastily arranged table. Four smaller tables had been pushed together to make one large enough to accommodate them.

Harrison explained the edict.

"Well," said Maggie, "that won't go down well!"

Abbud was to be brought to Government House.

The not-so-little cottage sat on the grass mound overlooking Kingston—the waters of Emily Bay were close by. It was a beautiful setting; one of the best gigs a government employee could get.

When Harrison was appointed for his two-year term, he had no idea what to expect. He thought he was going to a sleepy backwater. Little did he know that he would fall in love with the island and its people. Within three months, he had left the thoughts and chaos of city life behind him. He quickly knew he wanted to stay on Norfolk for the rest of his days.

Even the events of this week would not change his mind. If anything, it strengthened his resolve to stay. The island would need strong leadership in the months ahead.

A minibus pulled into the driveway. The gravel was noisy underneath the vehicle's tyres. Harrison was immediately on his feet. He peered out the window at the leader of the refugees. There was a look of defeat on Abbud's worn face.

The team of Navy SEALs escorted Abbud into the drawing room—it was the room used for official meetings. In the centre of the room was a wonderful old cedar wood table— an antique that had been brought to the island in the early 1900s.

"Please take a seat, Abbud." Harrison was gentle in his approach. He understood why the refugees had come here.

Nothing would explain their taking over the island. He understood fear, but the outcome could never be changed now.

"I have to tell you," Harrison began, "that Prime Minister Stephenson wants to make you an offer."

"Really?" Abbud was surprised. He had expected the navy ships would take them directly to Manus Island. There could be no other likely outcome, surely?

Harrison continued, "When you arrived on the island, we agreed to accept you as genuine refugees. You would have been processed accordingly."

Abbud nodded his agreement.

"This may have meant some time on Manus Island, but we could have expedited this." Harrison tried to show compassion.

"That was until you decided to take over this island and imprison the locals." Harrison could not help his rising anger. "Once you did that, you committed an act of terrorism."

Abbud's face drained of colour. *We are not terrorists!* he thought. He swallowed hard and then thought better of interrupting.

The chief minister looked Abbud squarely in the face. "You are all to be tried as terrorists under Australia's new terrorism laws."

"No!" Abbud insisted. "We were desperate, but we are not terrorists. We did not hurt anyone."

"Yes," Harrison affirmed. "you committed acts of terror by taking hostages and taking over the island."

The two men sat in thought.

"But you mentioned an offer?" Abbud was confused.

"That's right, Abbud." Harrison was unsure how it would be received.

"Prime Minister Stephenson is prepared to let you decide your fate. You can chose to either voluntarily transfer to Manus Island, OR you can leave Norfolk," Harrison started to explain.

"If you go to Manus, then proceedings will be started for your trial as terrorists – each and every one of you. When convicted—and you surely will be—the sentence will be life in prison. You will be incarcerated on Manus Island, in Papua New Guinea! You will never set foot in Australia." Harrison paused.

"However, if you decide to leave Norfolk of your own free will and sail away the way you came, you will be free to go—on one condition. You must agree never to return to any part of Australia. You will not even be allowed to stay in Australian waters. In fact, you would be escorted back out to international waters and tracked for some time. We must be sure you have left. You will be repelled if you try to return." The chief minister stared at Abbud.

Abbud hung his head low. *So that is the way of it?*

"I suppose I could not expect any more than that," Abbud eventually responded.

"So what is your decision?" Harrison thought he knew the answer.

"We will go." Abbud confirmed the expected response. "Could I please ask for one small consideration?"

"You can ask," Harrison responded, "though I cannot guarantee you will get a response that satisfies you. What's on your mind?"

"The body of the little boy who drowned—he needs to be buried." Abbud was troubled by the reality that one of their own had not been interred.

"Of course," Harrison replied in a softer tone. "We will see to it before your leave."

Burials on Norfolk followed a certain tradition. On average, there were only a handful of deaths each year—a result of a small population. There was no undertaker on the island—just not enough business to keep him busy.

This was a small community where everyone knew one another, so all got involved when one of their own had died. The locals always volunteered to dig the grave. The government normally supplied the coffin, but this time, one had to be specially crafted. It was rare to need a coffin so small.

Local women prepared the flowers—their gift to the family of the deceased. The minister would normally donate his time and prayers. The only cost to the family would be the purchase of a headstone when the ground had settled.

The island's cemetery took up an acre of land at the end of Quality Row, just before the road turned toward Bloody Bridge. It sat alongside the aptly named Cemetery Bay.

Today, the service would be conducted by the Islamic cleric, in a tongue that none of the locals understood. The little boy's parents stood by the small gravesite, devastation still showing in their demeanour. Nobody needed a translator to understand that. They had paid the ultimate price to try to attain freedom. The name Norfolk would remain with them forever.

Abbud and his wife stood at either side of the parents in a show of support. They tried to comfort them—a hopeless cause. These four, plus the cleric, were the only refugees allowed to attend. The others were still being detained.

Most of the locals had turned out to say good-bye to the little refugee who never made it ashore.

"So sad!" Maggie blubbered.

"Tragic!" Serena agreed as she wiped the tears from her eyes.

When the service was over, these two women moved forward to lay the flowers down on the newly dug earth. Then they decorated the grave with toys donated by the local children.

The Council of Nine had agreed to donate a headstone for the parents who could never again visit their infant son.

One by one, the vessels were filled with refugees. It took almost as long to load them as it had taken to unload them. Navy teams supervised the entire operation. The schooners were loaded with food and water as well as refugees.

To the north, in the waters of Cascade Bay, the first vessels prepared to leave Norfolk Island.

The refugees' schooners pulled up anchor and turned toward the east. A long line of schooners started the procession out of Australian waters. They were escorted by a contingent of Australian naval vessels.

Down at Kingston pier, Harrison was on hand to say farewell to Abbud. "Where will you go?" he asked his foreign friend.

"Cook Islands look good." Abbud smiled as the two shook hands.

Harrison felt a shiver down his spine.

16

RESOURCES

Prime Minister Stephenson announced the Australian government had approved massive investment in Norfolk Island infrastructure.

A grant of $80 million was established to build a harbour and port buildings at Slaughter Bay.

A formal protection squad was to be set up on Norfolk Island for a period of not less than five years.

The airport was to have formal surveillance established immediately. Up on Mount Pitt, the local radio and TV station infrastructure was to be fenced off—properly fenced this time.

The mobile network tower was included in this. All were to be enclosed with a three-metre-high concrete barrier fence topped with electrified fencing and CCTV.

Telecom's Anson Bay facility would receive the same treatment. It would also benefit from electronically controlled gates and electronic surveillance around the clock.

The *Norfolk Times* headlined, "Improved High-Speed Broadband to Improve Border Security Communications." The article went on to say, "This will improve response to disasters and emergencies." The locals took longer than the usual two minutes to read this edition.

Within weeks, infrastructure upgrades were started across the island. Local roads were repaired, and unsealed roads were tarred.

Lighting was installed along the main street of Burnt Pine Township. The cost of running it would be borne by the Australian government.

There would be greater mainland involvement in the running of the island in future.

Of course, there was a downside to all this investment. The locals were now required to pay income tax to the Australian government.

Norfolk Island's tourism board agreed to fund a new annual celebration. Their once-a-year Foundation Day Festival, held in March every year, would now be remembered with another annual carnival.

To be held at Kingston, the Day of Freedom celebrations were scheduled for April 1 each year.

ABOUT THE AUTHOR

Noleen Jordan spent twenty years in operations management and strategic sourcing for the entertainment, retail, and manufacturing industries. Now retired, she focuses on travelling and writing.

Her love of travel gave her the opportunity to experience many different cultures, providing her with knowledge that runs through both *Norfolk* and her previous crime thriller, *Shwedagon*.

She lives in Sydney, Australia, with her husband. They have three grown children and six grandchildren

15815709R00134

Printed in Great Britain
by Amazon